Helen Marr Bean

The Widow Wys

A Novel

Helen Marr Bean

The Widow Wys
A Novel

ISBN/EAN: 9783337030605

Printed in Europe, USA, Canada, Australia, Japan

Cover: Foto ©Andreas Hilbeck / pixelio.de

More available books at **www.hansebooks.com**

THE WIDOW WYSE

A Novel

"Oh, what a goodly outside falsehood hath!"
—Merchant of Venice

BOSTON
CUPPLES, UPHAM AND COMPANY
The Old Corner Bookstore
283 WASHINGTON STREET
1885

CONTENTS.

Chapter		Page
I.	MOBILE	1
II.	AT MADAM LEONARD'S	11
III.	SCHOOL LIFE CONTINUED	36
IV.	THE SOPHOMORES	52
V.	AT THE BREWSTERS'	60
VI.	THE WIDOW WYSE	87
VII.	GAYETIES	106
VIII.	AT MADAM LEONARD'S	110
IX.	COUNTRY GAYETIES	119
X.	RICHARD APTHORPE	129
XI.	HOLIDAY PLEASURES	147
XII.	MAJOR APTHORPE	161
XIII.	ALLIANCE	175
XIV.	PLANS AND PROJECTS	188
XV.	AT NEWPORT	215
XVI.	BACK TO MADAM LEONARD'S	222
XVII.	FAREWELL TO MADAM LEONARD'S	238
XVIII.	TRYING TO FORGET	245
XIX.	MAJOR APTHORPE'S QUEST	252
XX.	FOILED	255

THE WIDOW WYSE.

CHAPTER I.

MOBILE.

A TUMBLE, a roll, a bump, and a prolonged howl broke upon Miss Ethel Townsend's ear, one bright morning in September, as she was stepping from a long French-window to the veranda.

"Mercy on us!" she exclaimed, recognizing the voice and looking around.

"What's the matter, now, Dumps? How came you there?"

"Oh! Miss Teddy," cried poor Dumps at the foot of the stairs, "I 'ze dead, I 'ze dead, sure; specs I 'ze jes done gone an' killed myse'f."

A stout, comfortable-looking colored woman made her appearance at this moment, who called out: —

"Hyar, you, Dumps! go straight to de kitchen, an' doan go for to bodder Miss Teddy wid yer foolin's."

"You must n't scold the poor child, Dido," said Ethel. "Don't you see she has hurt herself?"

"She on'y wants a scuse for cryin', Miss Teddy," said Dido, coolly.

"Did n't go fur to do it, Miss Teddy," said Dumps. "'Clar' to goodness I did n't; jes stepped on de fust stair, an' down I come ker-blim. Oh! my pore ole bones."

Dumps was one of those children, who really delight in being unhappy, and was the butt of ridicule for the whole kitchen, and when she limped in with a doleful groan, saying, in imitation of her elders, "Oh! my pore ole bones," there was a shout of derisive laughter. It ceased, however, a moment after when Dido marched in with all the importance her position in the household gave her, saying, severely: —

"Specs yer'd laugh if de pore chile done broke her neck," and, with characteristic inconsistency, took Dumps in her arms and began rocking back and forth with the most tender expressions of compassion. Instantly there was a chorus of sympathetic voices.

"Whar's de camfire? Bring de arniky. De pore chile done hurt herse'f."

"Doan cry yer pore eyes out, honey," said Dido. "Kase yer's gwine Norf wid Miss Teddy, nex' week."

"I is?" said Dumps, starting up and rolling up the whites of her eyes in ecstasy, and forgetting to groan. "I is truly gwine Norf wid Miss Teddy? Bress my stars!"

It was an ideal Southern home, whose young mistress was fairly worshiped by her devoted servants. Ethel Townsend had beauty of a very striking order. She had inherited her mother's lovely golden-brown hair and all the grace for which that parent was famous. There was, however, no trace of the depressing languor which grew upon the mother until she lost her hold upon life altogether. Her father was a Northerner by birth, and from him came her glorious, dark eyes, her strong, good sense, and her abundant health. She was everything to him, as he was everything to her. He told her all his plans and projects, and she went to him with all her childish joys and sorrows. Neither of them ever thought of troubling the beautiful, frail mother. The father and daughter were constantly together. He took her with him on journeys by land and by sea. She tramped with him through marsh and wood after game, and was considered as good a shot as any young man in the country. She had an accomplished governess, and her father interested himself personally in her studies. But her lessons were constantly interrupted, and Dr. Townsend had felt for some time that his daughter needed the regular discipline of a boarding-school. Ethel was nearly seventeen when her mother died, and for months afterward the father and daughter wandered rest-lessly from place to place, when Dr. Townsend suddenly made up his mind that Ethel must go to school, and as he felt that he could not stay in Mobile without her, he decided to go abroad, and on the evening before our story opens he had returned from the North, where he had been to make arrangements for Ethel's comfort while finishing her studies. Acting upon the advice of a friend, he visited " Madam

Leonard's," the most refined and the most exclusive institution in the country. He found madam a tall, graceful lady, with a pale, clear-cut face, and engaging manners. She had occupied her present quarters for a year only. The house was large, and the grounds ample, with a background of pleasant woods a quarter of a mile away. High walls shut out the curious gaze of passers-by, but there was nothing to indicate its purpose to outsiders. It was the property of a gentleman then traveling in Europe, and had been occupied by him as a residence until leased to Madam Leonard.

"I am glad you came this morning," she said in her low, suave voice to Dr. Townsend, "for I do not allow myself to take more than eight young ladies, and I have seven already engaged. I take personal interest in each one, and consider them my guests, rather than my pupils. I have but few rules, and I make their duties as little irksome as possible. You may think my prices exorbitant, but when I tell you that I have resisted all inducements to take what are termed day-pupils, you will, I think, be quite satisfied. You see," she went on, with a smile of satisfaction, "that I have no outside influences to contend against; I watch over the young ladies as though they were my own daughters, and I consider this to be an absolutely safe place for any young girl."

"It is this very exclusiveness which pleases me," said Dr. Townsend. "I am sure Ethel ought to be happy here, but I beg you will remember that, owing to her mother's weak state for a long time before her death, she has been under very little restraint. Indeed, I am afraid she is a little spoiled. Your manner of living will, doubtless, be quite different to what she has been accustomed, and she will miss her home sorely " — his voice breaking a little. "Dear Madam Leonard, she is all I have; pray be patient with her, for I could not bear to think of my little girl as lonely or unhappy" —

"I quite understand," said Madam Leonard, in a sympathizing voice, "and I am sure you may trust me to make her sojourn with me both pleasant and profitable."

Then like the careful, loving father that he was, Dr. Townsend went into, and settled small details for his daughter's comfort. He asked many indulgences for her that Madam Leonard was loth to grant, but a persuasive voice which offered such generous pecuniary considerations could hardly be resisted by the impecunious widow, and Dr. Townsend went back to his Southern home well pleased with his daughter's prospects.

"I think you will like Madam Leonard, my dear," said he; "she is very pleasing in her manner, cordial, yet as dignified as a lady in her position should be. She has always moved in the best society, my friend Kennard tells me, but owing to reverses, followed by her husband's death, she has been compelled to do something for her own support. I should wish you to remember this, dear, for her position, at best, must be a trying one."

"I shall always try and do as you would wish to have me," answered Ethel. "I know that I disappointed you grievously, once upon a time."

"Yes," answered her father, laughing, "I am not likely to forget that. It was a clear case of obstinacy on your part, too. You should

have fulfilled my expectations, and proved
yourself a boy. However, I have my revenge
in calling you by the name you ought to
bear. You will never be anything but Teddy
to me."

"I remember," answered Ethel, "that you
taught me, when I was a very little girl, to say,
when asked my name, 'Dr. Edward Townsend,
junior.'"

"Yes," said he, "and you would have been
baptized by that name, but for ma's prejudices."

Then suddenly growing grave, he said : "All
this is nonsense, my darling, and I want you
always to remember that I am more than satisfied as it is ; I would not have it otherwise,
if I could."

Ethel patted his hand affectionately, saying,
"Oh! how I wish I could go with you!"

"I wish so, too," he answered, "with all my
heart ; but it would not be wise. Your education is by no means finished, and you could
hardly go to school after a year or two of
travel. Remain with Madam Leonard two
years, and after that time you shall go where
you will. I have made every arrangement

possible for your comfort. Dido will be near you to do everything in the way of washing and mending. She will have a little white cottage that will delight her heart. I had a little difficulty in accomplishing this, for madam's rules are very strict with regard to outsiders, but she yielded finally. You must see her often, so she won't grow homesick, and, I am sure," he went on, with a smile of intense amusement, "that Dumps will cheer you up when you feel lonesome. Write me as freely as you talk to me, my dear, and if I have left anything undone, let me know it at once. I saw Jack Fenton in New York. He goes back to the university soon, and will be quite near you. Indeed, I think you may be able to see the tops of the buildings from your chamber windows. At any rate, they are not far away."

"It will seem like a bit of home to see Jack," answered Ethel, "and I cannot be too thankful for Dido and poor Dumps. How thoughtful you are for me!"

"That is what I am living for," said her father. "It is my greatest pleasure to make you happy. You will feel the necessary restraint at first, of course, but I hope it will not prove very irksome to you."

"Oh! I shall not mind it at all," said Ethel. "I mean to study faithfully, and I shall not have time to be unhappy."

The next week was a busy one for Ethel. Old friends — of whom she had many — must be visited and taken leave of, and arrangements made for the poor people whom she had relieved and comforted for so many years. There was weeping and wailing among the faithful colored people about her, in view of her departure. Dido, alone, was proud and happy, and poor Dumps was almost cheerful.

CHAPTER II.

"DEAREST PAPA, — You will doubtless be surprised at this added syllable, but you must know that your daughter has been laughed at. Yes, actually laughed at, on account of her paws. I did not know what it all meant, until Kitty Brewster, my roommate, a kind-hearted Boston girl, explained it to me. So it seems that I have to choose between 'par' and papa. The former being detestable, I choose the latter. Never expect to hear me say 'paw' again.

"I am sure, dear papa, that you will want to know, first of all, my impressions concerning Madam Leonard's. You know its pleasant surroundings, and have seen its mistress; but you must pardon me if I say that I do not think that a man's perceptions are quite as quick as a woman's — at least where women are concerned.

"Now, you are laughing at me, and I hear you

say : 'She does not like her'; but no matter.
I shall say nothing of Madam Leonard at
present, having seen but little of her.

" Miss Carpenter seems to manage everything,
and she seems happy only when she can thwart
some pet plan of the young ladies; so, of
course, they all hate her.   Miss Eliza, her
sister, a little, meek, old, young woman, is
her echo.   I think she would be kind to us
if she dared.   She does not look as though
she ever thoroughly enjoyed anything in the
whole course of her life.   Our German professor is a poor man, with a large family.   He
looks as though it was a struggle to maintain
them; but he is considered a good teacher.
You will feel gratified to know that he compli-
ments your daughter on her proficiency in his
native tongue.   He teaches other branches,
also.   I have just begun Italian, which I like
very much.   Miss Carpenter has the French
classes ; but Madam Leonard is looking for
a native teacher.   I hope she will soon find
one, for, although, as you know, I have no need
to study that language, I do want the girls to
have a better teacher.

"Kitty Brewster, as I told you, is from Boston. She does not wear spectacles, but she is just as 'nice' as she can be. Very pretty, too, although she does not think so. She calls her face common, because she is neither a decided blonde, nor yet a brunette, and can wear one color as well as another. The Brewsters live in fine style in Boston, and are very wealthy, Lizzie Highgate says, and one can see that they must be cultivated, as well; though Lizzie says nothing about that, as she worships wealth and cares very little for culture. Thanks to you, we have two bedrooms and a private parlor, so we are what Lizzie Highgate calls 'quite swell.' I wonder what Madam Leonard would say if she could hear this young lady's slang? Yet she is clearly madam's favorite. She is a little, black-tressed creature, with large, dark eyes and pale face. We call her 'The Little Gypsy,' and she makes the most of her dark beauty by dressing in the most dashing style. She is as fond of colors as Dido, only I should not dare to say so in her hearing, for she has a temper that is far from angelic, and displays it upon the slightest provocation. She lives in a little town farther North.

"Edith Preble is from Portland, Maine. A tall, stately girl, with a fine, proud face. I like her, but she is not a favorite, being rather reserved, and very unyielding where right and wrong are concerned, and she never needs to be reproved. The girls say that she was never known to miss a lesson, and is always provokingly correct in her deportment. ('A fine example for you, my dear,' I hear you say.) Lizzie Highgate says that her father is poor, and that she has been foolish enough to engage herself to a young lawyer, of her own city, as poor as herself. I suggested to Miss Highgate that possibly they were going to marry for love, and she answered: 'Nonsense!' The other girls are younger, and do not particularly interest me.

"Now, papa, dear, you are to keep these young ladies in your mind, for I shall have nothing else to write about, and you promised to be interested in whatever concerns me. I got your note from New York, and am anxiously awaiting a letter from across the ocean. I have cried but once since you left me. It was last evening, when Dido said: 'Say howdy to yer paw, honey, and tell him we's satisfied.' Miss Carpenter would like to keep me from going there, but she cannot. I think I know your daughter well enough to promise that. But Kitty is getting impatient (you are to love Kitty), and, I am sure, she cannot keep her tongue quiet much longer, so I will say good-by. From your loving

"TEDDY."

"My dear Ethel, I am thankful that you have at last finished that interminable letter," remarked the aforesaid Kitty. "What can you possibly find to write about? Letter-writing is my pet aversion. I have been dying to talk to you for the last half-hour."

"Well, my friend, don't lose time, now you have the opportunity," said Ethel. "Talk away; but first tell me what you do with yourselves on Saturdays."

"Oh! we do our mending,—I mean those of us who are obliged to (you should thank your stars that you are not),—and write letters, as you have been doing, until it is time to go for our walk."

"Do you have any particular time for walking?" asked Ethel, eagerly; "if not, let us go now. I am longing for the woods. It must be lovely there."

"You poor, little innocent," said Kitty, in a pitying tone. "Do you imagine for a moment that our ancient grimalkin will permit us to go when and where we please, and without her detested presence?" ·

"You don't mean to say that Miss Carpenter will accompany us?" said Ethel.

"Not only Miss Carpenter, but **Miss Eliza** also," answered **Kitty**, enjoying Ethel's ludicrous look of disgust.

"In the first place," Kitty went on, "we set out in pairs, like convicts, with a keeper at the head — that's **Miss** Eliza, and another at the foot to take us all in — that's Miss Carpenter" —

"But what is it all for?" interrupted Ethel.

"To see that we keep step," said Kitty, coolly, "and that we do not raise our voices above the conventional society standard, and that we do not laugh. We can smile occasionally, but not too often, and, above all things, to protect us should we meet a man."

"Meet a man?" repeated Ethel, in a bewildered tone.

"Yes, my lambkin, 'meet a man.' In case we do, you must immediately drop your eyes to the ground. You must, on no account, lift so much as an eye-winker."

"How perfectly absurd you are this morning, Kitty! Do be sensible, if you can, and tell me if we have to submit to strict discipline on holidays," said Ethel.

"I have told you the solemn truth," answered Kitty, "and if you do not believe me, wait and see."

"It is too ridiculous to believe," said Ethel.

Just then a bell rang.

"That means that we are to prepare for our walk," said Kitty, rising.

"I would rather not go," said Ethel, decidedly.

"Oh! but you must," answered Kitty. "They won't let you off. Come, get your hat. It won't be so very disagreeable, after all. We will walk together, and talk so that the rest won't hear."

They set out ten minutes later, and had

nearly reached the woods, where they would be allowed to separate a little, when Ethel noticed a dogcart, in which were seated two young men, coming rapidly toward them.

"Drop your eyes, dear," said Kitty, mischievously, as they were passing.

"One of them was Lizzie Highgate's brother, but she could n't speak to him."

"And the other," said Ethel, eagerly, "was Jack Fenton, an old friend of mine, whom you must know."

"Hush!" said Kitty, warningly, "the old cat will hear."

Just then, they reached the woods, and Miss Carpenter gathered the young ladies about her, and said, in measured tones : —

"I noticed that one of the young ladies held a handkerchief in her hand, while those young men were passing. She should have known better." Miss Eliza heaved a deep sigh, as Miss Carpenter went on,

"I will not accuse her of doing so indelicate a thing as waving that — that — suggestive article; but I noticed that the young men were encouraged to bow in the most impressive manner."

Miss Eliza almost groaned.

"It must have been out of respect for you, Miss Carpenter," said Lizzie Highgate, quickly, the owner of the above-mentioned handkerchief.

Miss Carpenter coughed dryly, and said: —

"We will give the young lady the benefit of the doubt; but I would suggest that hereafter no young lady permit herself to be seen, while walking, with a handkerchief in her hand, excepting under the most pressing circumstances."

There were signs of a struggle between amusement and indignation in Ethel Townsend's face; but she made no remark; and they were soon gathering handfuls of brilliant autumn leaves, wherewith to decorate their rooms for the coming winter. It was a glorious October morning, and the girls soon forgot their annoyances, and chatted gayly with each other, thoroughly enjoying the clear air and bright sunshine, and they went back refreshed in body and mind.

"It wasn't so bad, after all?" queried Kitty.

"It was perfectly delightful — after we got

there," said Ethel. "And won't these leaves brighten up our rooms? I'll have Dido press them to-night."

"Oh! most fortunate girl, to possess a Dido," answered Kitty, with a sigh.

"Oh! I couldn't live without Dido," said Ethel, decidedly. "You cannot think what a helpless, useless creature I have always been, with half a dozen servants to wait especially on me. Why, I never did a thing for myself in my life, until I came here. I shall never forget, you dear child, how patiently you have taught me, morning after morning, to dress my hair. I really think I am getting to be quite 'dexterious,' as Dido would say."

"Your hair is perfectly lovely, and you do it beautifully," said Kitty, enthusiastically.

"I will have Dido press all the leaves, if you think the girls would like it," said Ethel.

"'Like it!'" repeated Kitty; "they would go down on their knees to you, every one of them."

Later in the afternoon, as Ethel was preparing to visit Dido, she met Madam Leonard, and, as she greeted her in her pleasant way, Ethel said : —

"I suppose I may go over to the cottage for a little while, madam?"

"My dear child," answered madam, in her soft voice, "I wanted to speak to you about those colored people. I don't like to deny you anything; but I hope you will not ask to go there quite as often as you have done; they are hardly fit associates for you."

Ethel looked at her in amazement, as she answered: —

"I thought I was to go there when I pleased. I am sure papa understood it so. He particularly told me not to let Dido get homesick."

"Yes, dear," answered madam, patting Ethel softly on the shoulder. "I am willing that you should go there, only not quite so often. You were there last evening, and the child will be here to-night for your linen."

"Oh! yes," said Ethel, impatiently, "but Dumps doesn't signify. I want to see Dido about pressing my leaves; besides, I promised to write a letter for her. I didn't have time last night."

"'Dumps,'" repeated Madam Leonard,

"what a strange name! Has the child no other?"

"Oh! yes, I suppose so," said Ethel, carelessly; "I will inquire if you like."

"And she has always lived in your family?" said madam, significantly. "Do you not think that she should be taught that she is a responsible human being? Did you never try to teach the poor thing?"

"Oh! yes," answered Ethel, "I tried all last winter to teach her to say: 'Sin is an abomination unto the Lord'; and in the spring, as she had only got to 'Sin is a bodderation,' I gave it up. But she goes to school now, and she has really learned a good deal. The last time I was there, she exclaimed, eagerly, as soon as she saw me: —

"'Oh! Miss Teddy, I can spell spoon.'

"'Well, Dumps, spell spoon,' said I.

"She took a spoon from the table and spelled, 'J. C-a-r-t-e-r, spoon.' I was really proud of her. I was, indeed."

Madam coughed, gently, as she said: "Well, dear, you may go for an hour. Pray, be back punctually."

She was always gentle and gracious to the young ladies, leaving all the disagreeables to Miss Carpenter.

On Sunday mornings they went to church. The dear, old rector was one of Madam Leonard's friends, and, as he was not considered dangerous, being over seventy, was a welcome visitor at all times.

The young ladies were very fond of him, for, though a little prosy in his sermons, he was a delightful companion and a wise counsellor. In the afternoon came Bible-lessons at home, and in the evening the girls wrote letters.

One morning Lizzie Highgate came rushing into the young ladies' parlor, with scarcely an apology for a knock, saying to Kitty, who was the only visible occupant of the room :—

" Do we have extra pages of Roman history to-day? It would be just like Miss Carpenter to give us a page or two in addition because it was so hard we could n't get it yesterday. I asked Ethel Townsend at breakfast, and she answered: 'Reckon.' I wonder why she is always 'reckoning.'"

" For the same reason," said Ethel, straight-

ening up from behind a large easy-chair, where
she had been sitting on a low stool, "that you
are always 'guessing.' "

Lizzie reddened deeply.

" How strangely our peculiarities strike each
other," she went on, sweetly. "Now, for a long
time I could not get accustomed to this constant guessing. I said to myself: 'They do
not seem to really *know* anything.' Only
this morning our friend here" — turning to
Kitty — "was asked if she would have more
steak, and she answered: 'No, I guess not.'
And I thought : 'How strange that she should
n't *know !* ' "

With her feathers all ruffled, and her small
nose in the air, Miss Highgate turned to go,
saying, primly : —

" I beg your pardon, Miss Townsend.   I did
not know you were there ; " and Ethel called
after her : —

" Perhaps I ought to beg your pardon,
although I did know that you were there.
We have half a page of history extra."

"What made you answer her so, Ethel?"
asked Kitty.

" Could n't help it, my dear," answered Ethel.
" I never like to lose an opportunity, and you
must admit that she gave me provocation
enough."

"Yes," answered Kitty, "but she won't get
over it for a week, and I particularly wanted to
ask a favor of her."

"Well, why not ask it?" replied Ethel.
"She cannot be angry with you, as you said
nothing."

"Oh! you hardly know Miss Highgate,"
answered Kitty. "She does not stop to dis-
criminate when she is in her tantrums. It is
quite enough for her that I was with you when
this happened."

"What a strange girl she is!" said Ethel.
" I am sure I am glad to be told of my faults,
and if Lizzie had spoken to me instead of to
you, I should have thanked her. I acknowledge that darkeyisms are bad enough ; but you
must pardon me if I say that Yankeeisms
seem infinitely worse to me. But there is
one thing that I cannot get accustomed to,
and that is Lizzie Highgate's slang phrases.
For instance : I borrowed a pencil of her

yesterday, having mislaid my own, and, after
using it, I handed it back, saying, 'Thank
you, very much.' Instead of taking it, she
answered, without looking up, 'Oh! shoot
the pencil!' The window being open, I did
as she requested. I 'shot the pencil' out of
the window, and, if you will believe me, she
was angry."

Kitty laughed, saying, "She does use a
dreadful amount of slang; but she has brothers,
my dear, and 'brothers are awful,' she says;
they talk nothing but slang. She will go to
her room now, and tear around for half an
hour; after that, she will feel better."

"I do hope," said Ethel, laughingly, "that
she won't tear her clothes. I never saw anybody's raiment so pinned together in my life.
She must use all her pin-money for its legiti-
mate purpose. I don't believe she ever takes
a stitch."

"She only mends what will be likely to come
under Miss Carpenter's eye," said Kitty.
"She has no time. She takes it all to dress
her hair. She gets up at six o'clock every
morning and works upon it until breakfast-

time. Personal adornment is Miss Highgate's pet weakness."

" I knew that it must take time and patience to dress hair in that impossible sort of style," said Ethel. " I have often wondered at the structure; but I did not think her equal to the sacrifice of her morning nap for any purpose whatsoever."

" She is as vain as a peacock," answered Kitty. " We roomed together last year, and she used to awaken me sometimes by slamming around because she could n't get her jetty locks to suit her; and one morning in particular, I remember, I was dreadfully annoyed, and said: ' Lizzie, why don't you swear outright and be done with it ? '

" ' What do you mean ? ' " she asked, sharply, her nose in the air. ' There 's many an oath in the slam of a door.' I quoted. ' You must have slammed several into your bureau-drawers this morning. I think you would feel a greater relief in doing as I suggested; that is all.' She did n't speak to me for a week.

" It is fortunate for Lizzie," resumed Kitty, after a pause, "that Madam Leonard does not

interfere with our clothes. Indeed, I think
she likes to have us dress. It was not allowed
at all at Miss Moran's, where I was sent several years ago."

"Did you all dress alike?" asked Ethel,
with a look of horror. "I thought such
things were practised only in charity-schools."

"Not precisely alike," answered Kitty;
"but our dresses were perfectly plain; an overskirt was considered an abomination. We
were obliged to brush back our hair, and do it
in the simplest manner possible; and not
a particle of jewelry was allowed, not even a
plain ring. I remember, when I was there,
that Miss Moran was very much troubled about
one of the girls who wore a ring that was put
upon her finger years before, and she could not
get it off. She made her soak her hand in
warm, soapy water, but to no purpose, and
she was forced to let her wear it."

"I wouldn't have remained there a day,"
said Ethel, indignantly.

"I am sure you would not," said Kitty.
"She would have swept your dainty ruffles
and delicate laces into your boxes at once,

and you would not have seen them again, until you got home. One must be 'plain behind and plain before' at Miss Moran's."

"Then, this isn't the worse place in the world?" queried Ethel, doubtfully.

"It is a paradise compared with Miss Moran's," said Kitty.

But, notwithstanding Kitty's prediction concerning the length of Miss Highgate's fit of temper, that young lady met her a few hours after, with her face wreathed in smiles. She held up a letter with a foreign postmark, saying, —

"See! I have a letter from my dearest friend. And only think! she tells me she will be here by Easter. I shall begin to be home-sick as soon as I know she has arrived."

"We cannot allow that, my child," said the soft voice of Madam Leonard, who at that moment appeared. "But how is my dear Julia?"

"Very well, and very impatient to see us all, she says," answered the radiant Lizzie.

"Dear girl!" said Madam Leonard, "how much we all want to see her! She was my first pupil," she continued, turning to Ethel, "and I am very much attached to her. She married soon after she left me, and in six months became a widow. She has seen much trouble, but she bears it all with uncommon sweetness."

"She was always charming," said Lizzie; "but, I suppose, she will come back more fascinating than ever, if possible. She has been admired immensely abroad; but, judging from her letters, she is not in the least spoiled."

"You are very enthusiastic concerning your friend, my dear," said madam, smiling, "and, I am sure, you have reason to be; she is very dear to us all."

Kitty raised her eyebrows at this, while Lizzie read from the letter:—

"'The first moment I can spare from dearest mamma, I shall go to my dear Madam Leonard.'"

Madam flushed with pleasure, as she answered:—

"Her devotion to her mother is one of the most beautiful traits of her character."

Ethel noticed that Kitty not only raised her

eyebrows at this, but her expressive shoulders, as well; but she did not speak. When they were alone she asked: —

"Who is this remarkable person, whom Madam Leonard and Miss Highgate vie with each other in praising?"

"Oh! have n't you heard of her before?" said Kitty. "I am surprised. She is the Widow Wyse, whom madam is always holding up for an example, and to whom Lizzie writes long, gushing letters. She has had a minute description of you, my dear, long before this, with Miss Highgate's own personal opinion of you. She writes regularly, once a fortnight, giving her all the gossip. She receives very irregular replies, but Lizzie is more than satisfied, for she knows that her beloved Julia is so admired, and so overwhelmed with attentions, and is in such a whirl of gayety all the time, that she cannot possibly find time to write oftener, but when she does write to her 'dear little Wild Rose' she tells her that she is never absent from her thoughts, and that she would be perfectly happy if said 'Wild Rose' were with her, and I am sure I wish she was with all my heart, for I

am quite as tired of her as I am of the Widow
Wyse."

"Why do you call her 'the Widow Wyse'?"
said Ethel, laughing.

"Owing to the natural depravity of my
nature," answered Kitty; "she does n't like it,
and it makes Lizzie furious."

"So you know her personally?"

"Oh! yes," answered Kitty, "I know her very
well. You see, sister Margaret, Mrs. Onslow,
lives in Alliance, a part of the time, as her husband has large manufacturing interests there,
and Mrs. Houlton, Mrs. Wyse's mother, lives
there too, so it was Mrs. Wyse's former home.
It is Lizzie's home too, and it was upon the
widow's recommendation that she came to
Madam Leonard's. Alliance is a lovely place,
and as Margaret is rather lonely there, I generally visit her in June, and sometimes in September. She is at the seashore during July and
August, and she spends the winter in Boston,
coming down about Thanksgiving time. I want
you to know Margaret. She is charming, and
dear little Gertrude is a lovely child. You will
see them before long at our house, and we

will visit her just as soon as Madam Leonard dismisses us for the summer."

"You plan beautifully for me, Kitty," said Ethel; "but are you allowed to select your sister's guests?"

"My sister will be more than glad to have you with her, so you need not say a word or make a plan. Everything has been arranged: mamma and I have planned fully for our holidays and summer vacation. You are to spend Thanksgiving, Christmas, and the Easter holidays with me in Boston, June at Alliance with Margaret, July and August at our country-place, which is lovely, and September — well, we hardly know what we will do with September until it comes. It is a lovely month to travel. If you have thought for a moment that I could have the heart to leave you in this forlorn place and go back to my dear, delightful old home, it only shows that you don't know Kitty Brewster. And now, my dear Miss Townsend, allow me to inform you that it is high time you were studying."

Ethel gave her vivacious little friend a grateful kiss, and obediently took up her book.

After an hour's study, during which time neither of the girls spoke a word, Ethel started up suddenly, saying, "I cannot understand why Jack Fenton does n't call upon me. I think it is very shabby of him. I want so much to introduce him to you."

Kitty laughed outright : indeed, she seemed so much amused that Ethel was annoyed and said : "I don't know what you are laughing at, Kitty; it seems hardly polite."

"I beg your pardon," answered Kitty, still laughing, "but you are such an amazing piece of innocence that I positively cannot help it. You are so infantile in your ideas, my child, it is perfectly delicious. You think you can have whatever you cry for."

"And you are so enigmatical in your talk," retorted Ethel, "that I cannot understand you at all. Will you condescend to explain?"

Kitty assumed a pitying smile as she answered : "If you have imagined for a moment that you will be permitted to see one of the young men belonging to that institution," pointing to the university buildings, "you will be disappointed."

"Do you mean to say," said Ethel, "that Madam Leonard would not allow me to see Jack, if he called?"

"I do mean to say just that," answered Kitty.

A dangerous light came into Ethel's eyes, as she said, in a low tone: "Kitty, if Jack Fenton, my old friend and neighbor calls here, I shall see him. Do you mark what I say? *I shall see him.*"

Kitty shook her head, and at that moment a class-bell rang.

CHAPTER III.

SCHOOL LIFE CONTINUED.

ONE Saturday afternoon, a few weeks later, as Ethel was looking aimlessly out of the window, she saw young Fenton coming briskly up the walk. In an instant her listlessness was gone. She sprang up and, girl-like, threw a hasty glance into the mirror, saying, "There's Jack, at last," and started toward the door. She heard him ask for her, and he was invited into the drawing-room. But, instead of calling her, the servant called Miss Carpenter, who said a few words to her visitor, and dismissed him. Ethel could hardly believe her senses, notwithstanding what Kitty had said. In an instant she was at the front-door, in which stood Miss Carpenter.

"That was my visitor," said Ethel, in a low tone.

"Yes," answered Miss Carpenter, coolly, "but the young ladies are not permitted to receive visits from young gentlemen,"—raising her arm to bar the way. "Go to your room, Miss Townsend."

"Stand out of my way," said Ethel, fiercely pushing her arm aside as she walked out of the door, calling after the fast-disappearing Jack, leaving Miss Carpenter the picture of angry amazement.

"You poor, little nun," said Jack, smiling, and taking the hand she offered. "How did you manage to escape? Joe Highgate offered to bet that I would n't be able to catch even a glimpse of you, but I thought I would make the attempt. What a dragon that woman is! I thought she would bite my head off, when I asked for you. Was it Madam Leonard?"

"Oh, no," answered Ethel, recovering her voice, "Madam Leonard is a lady, at least in appearance. It was Miss Carpenter, and she *is* an 'old dragon.' I was determined to see you, especially after she told me, with so much apparent enjoyment, that I could n't," she went on rapidly; "but I am too angry to talk to you. I wonder I did n't strike her."

"You poor child," said Jack, "what will she do to you for your disobedience?"

"Oh, I don't know, and, for that matter, I don't care," said Ethel, recklessly. "She will shut me up, and keep me on bread and water, perhaps. Fancy papa's daughter in that condition!"

"But your father expected me to call upon you, I am sure," said Jack. "He spoke about it in New York."

"Poor, dear pa," answered Ethel. "How angry he would be if he knew of this. I wonder if I should be permitted to see him? No, I am not to see you or anybody else. I say it's a shame, a perfect outrage!" she went on, vehemently. "I have a great mind to rebel."

"I don't know what you call this," said Jack, laughing. "I should call it rebellion, with a vengeance."

"So it is," answered Ethel, "and I am glad of it ; but I must go back. Good-by!" and back she ran. As she turned toward the house, her eye caught the flutter of a white handkerchief at one of the upper windows, and behind it Lizzie Highgate's gypsy face, and she said to herself, while her lip curled with scorn : "That's Miss Highgate's idea of propriety."

Miss Carpenter met her at the door, saying, in her primmest manner : —

" You may go to your room, Miss Townsend, and remain there while I confer with Madam Leonard."

Ethel looked at her with stormy eyes, but she did not reply, as she passed on to her room, which she reached full of wrath and indignation. She expected to find Kitty and to pour her woes into her sympathetic ear, but Miss Carpenter had taken care that Ethel should be left quite alone until she was summoned to the dread presence of Madam Leonard.

But after learning of Ethel's unheard-of disobedience, that politic woman was completely at a loss as to what it was best to do. She knew that Ethel would not bear any very humiliating punishment, and she was far too profitable a pupil to lose. Sending Miss Carpenter to her duties, she pondered deeply upon the subject, and at last decided that her refractory pupil must be conciliated, however mortifying it might be. Pulling the bell-rope at her side, madam said to the servant who answered it : —

" Go to Miss Townsend's room, and ask her

if she will be kind enough to come to me into
the library."

Ethel obeyed the polite summons, and was
met at the door by Madam Leonard.

"I am very sorry for this, my child," she said,
with a sorrowful smile.

Ethel's eyes blazed, but she did not speak.
She was too angry.

"Sit down, my dear, and let us talk it over.
You must not think that I do not know just
how you feel: I do know all about it, and I
sympathize with you too.   Yes, dear, I do,"
she repeated, seeing an incredulous look in
Ethel's eyes, "although it may be hard for you
to think so. You see, Ethel," she went on,
artfully, "that, while I would do anything in
my power to make you happy, I must maintain
the dignity of my household. You cannot see
any reason why you should not receive a call
from your young friend, and under other circumstances there would be none.   But put yourself
in my place, for a moment, if you can. What
would be the result of my permitting such
a thing? Would not the other young ladies
insist upon the same privilege? Would Lizzie

Highgate, or Kitty Brewster, or Edith Preble, say, smilingly: 'It is perfectly proper for Ethel Townsend to receive the young collegians but it would not be proper for me'? You know they would not. Why, my dear child," she went on, with engaging sweetness, "I have not a plain or uninteresting young lady in my house. Ah! how I should like to bring you all out, if I were in society, and if I should open my house to the students, it would be overrun with them," and here she ventured to pat Ethel's hand gently. "Ethel, dear, don't you see I could n't do it?"

"But papa invited him to call upon me," said Ethel, her anger fast dying out.

"Yes, dear," answered Madam Leonard, "I do not doubt that at all, but he did not understand the difficulties in the case. I am sure he would sustain me if he did."

"Perhaps he would," answered Ethel, candidly; "but why should Miss Carpenter treat us as she does? She takes every opportunity to be disagreeable, and we all detest her for it."

"Detest is a strong word, my dear," said Madam Leonard, smiling. "But did it ever

occur to you that she might be one of my trials,
too? You have had a great trial to-day, and I
am showing you both sympathy and confidence
in speaking in this way. I should not dare to
speak of Miss Carpenter as I have done to anybody else in the house." And she spoke truly.
She knew that Ethel was the soul of honor.
"She is a fine scholar, and an able teacher, and
is invaluable to me in many ways. I do not
think I could find anybody to quite fill her
place. When I first received young ladies in
this way I had a charming young teacher whom
they all loved, but I found after a while that
they did not get on as they ought, and, upon
investigation, I discovered that she not only
was not sufficiently learned herself, but that
she had not the gift of imparting to others
what she did know, so I was obliged to dismiss
her. Miss Carpenter came to me with the
highest testimonials, and I engaged her at
once. She is not very amiable, I know, but she
suits me in other respects, so I do not like to
give her up;" and seeing that Ethel was in a
very different frame of mind to when she entered, she thought it safe to dismiss her, which
she did with these words: —

"Now, my dear, I am going to recommend a dose of medicine. What should a little girl, who has disobeyed, and been let off with a short lecture, do?"

Ethel looked up inquiringly.

"She can do no less than apologize, can she?"

"Do you mean that I shall write a note to Miss Carpenter?" asked Ethel.

"I will leave it entirely with you, Ethel," said Madam Leonard, knowing very well that Ethel would do as she desired.

Ethel went to her room, but she was hardly satisfied.

"I don't know what makes me distrust Madam Leonard so," she said to herself. "What she says seems reasonable enough. All the same, I don't like her. I feel as though I ought to keep saying, 'From hatred and malice and all uncharitableness,' etc. I'll write to papa. He understands me better than anybody else." And seizing her pen, she wrote:—

"My Dear Papa,—You have called me, many times, a clear-headed young lady. Well, do you know that I sometimes wish that I were

a little stupid, like other people. I should then
be considered much more amiable and charitable than I am at present. I am not trying
to mystify you, but shall come to the point at
once. I wish I had no doubts about Madam
Leonard. You thought her charming, and are,
no doubt, secretly hoping that your daughter
may grow to be like her. Heaven forbid!
The other young ladies think her sweet and
lovely. They grow very enthusiastic over her,
and wonder at my coldness on the subject.
They are equally agreed in detesting Miss
Carpenter. Now there is no doubt at all
about Miss Carpenter's being detestable; but
the question will keep rising in my mind,
whether Madam Leonard is not equally so.
Miss Carpenter surely does not make the rules.
They are made by madam herself, and it is safe
to conclude that they are carried out by her
orders, and I can say truly that they are
carried out with a vengeance. ' Eternal vigi-
lance' is Miss Carpenter's motto; she is faithful to her employer, which is the only admi-
rable thing about her. But what seems strange
to me is the superficial way in which the

young ladies look at this matter; at least, all but Edith Preble, who says very little. She is engaged, and does n't seem to care for small annoyances. Kitty proposes that we all get engaged, and then we shall see nothing but the faces of our beloved ones, and shall not need to be watched. But this is a digression.

"To go back to Madam Leonard : she seems to me just like those high-toned politicians we know of, who employ those beneath them socially to do their dirty work — a cold, calculating woman, with 'a hand of iron and a heart of steel.' I sometimes wonder if she ever felt one generous impulse. Going to her from my warm-hearted, generous, impulsive Kitty is like foolishly eating an ice after a hot dinner. It strikes a chill to one's very marrow. I feel a chill creep into my heart whenever I approach her, and it remains while I am in her presence. I am rather glad to write this instead of saying it, for you would interrupt me with questions and apologies for madam, and otherwise distract me, and you know that I am never satisfied until I have 'said my say.'

"There is another thing that I cannot understand, and that is our proximity to the university. Kitty says that it is because two or three of the girls have brothers there, and their parents persuaded madam to change her residence, which was formerly near Philadelphia. But it can hardly be for that reason, since the students are not allowed to call upon the young ladies upon any pretext whatsoever, neither are we allowed to go where we shall be likely to meet them. What will you think when I tell you that I was forbidden to see Jack Fenton this afternoon? I did see him, however, but it was by wilful disobedience, for which I am in disgrace. I have been lectured by madam, and I must write a note of apology to Miss Carpenter for defying her authority, but I fancy it will not be very satisfactory to her. What do you think about it?

"Oh! yes, dear papa, this is undoubtedly a 'safe place for girls.' But you must not think me unhappy. Indeed, I think I rather enjoy this new experience. It is an amazing experience I assure you; for it gives me an opportunity to study different characters, —

unusual characters, — it seems to me. And
then I have something to look forward to, for
every day brings us nearer to that blessed, old
Yankee feast-day — Thanksgiving. I am to
spend that and the three following days with
Kitty in Boston.

" You cannot think how kind the Brewsters
are to your daughter. Mrs. Brewster came to
see Kitty last week, and brought the loveliest
flowers; you can imagine how I reveled in
them. She is a charming woman, and she
invited me, in the warmest manner, to visit
them. She idolizes Kitty, and Kitty loves me,
so you see I am in an enviable position. Dido
is in despair because she cannot cook my
Thanksgiving dinner. She seems contented,
and always says: 'Say howdy to yer paw,'
— but poor Dumps; you would laugh to hear
her go on. She says: 'Dis yer Norf is drefful
fur de mizzry in my head, and my pore ole
bones.' She says that I shall send her home
in a little box, and I shall hear her bones rattle
round like peas in a pod. When I get low-
spirited I go to see her, and she does really
cheer me up, as you predicted. She is very

bright, and so ridiculously solemn, and makes such droll speeches, that no one could help laughing at her.

"How strange that you should run across 'the Widow Wyse,' as Kitty calls her. She was Madam Leonard's pet pupil, and Lizzie Highgate's most intimate friend, so we hear a good deal about her. You did not say whether you were favorably impressed by her or not. I hope not, for I am sure I should not like her. I hear you say: 'Could prejudice go farther?' All the same, your Teddy is almost always right.

"Mrs. Brewster writes that your friend, Richard Apthorpe, returned last week, so I suppose you did not meet him as you hoped. Kitty says that he is very clever and very critical, and that she is awfully afraid of him. She says that I shall be sure to meet him, as he and her mamma are the best of friends. Now, is it not very sweet of Kitty to invite me to her home? Such a rest as it will be from Madam Leonard's.

"Your letters are such a comfort to me ; you would laugh, I am sure, if you could know how

many times I have read your last. Indeed, I
do not know myself. I take a peep into it
whenever I get a moment's time. I like your
way of writing letters — jotting down interesting things as they occur, like keeping a journal. And this reminds me of my promise
to you when you left me.

"Now, dear papa, I cannot understand why
you should wish me to keep a journal. In
the first place it is mighty hard (a darkeyism),
and I have been trying to find a sufficient
excuse for not doing it. And I must tell you
of one which came to me yesterday, in the
shape of a story — a true one, told by Lizzie
Highgate.

"It seems that one of her acquaintances,
a lady prominent in society, had for years kept
a diary of the smallest events concerning her
household matters. Of the expenses, and the
trouble she had in getting the necessary
money from 'that stingy man' to meet them.
Of the frequent quarrels between herself and
'that horrid man.' Of her joy when the
'hateful old bear' went away, and of the peacefulness which came over the household in

consequence of his absence; and of the trials, troubles, and tribulations of married life generally. All of which was true, no doubt, and it must have been a great relief to the poor woman's overburdened soul thus to confide in her dumb friend, the journal. And it would have been all right, and a great comfort for her to read over, and thus bring often to mind the cruelties practised upon an amiable and, of course, inoffensive woman. But alas! one day, after tiring herself to death cutting out garments for the poor, — she was very charitable withal, — she drew from its hiding-place the beloved journal, and, after reading a few lines let it drop into her lap, while her thoughts (probably) went back to the days of her girlhood, with scores of lovers to choose from, any one of whom — well! well! well! how her thoughts flew from one to another, when the doorbell rang. There was a summons to the drawing-room, and madam, rising hastily, let the journal fall among the cuttings at her feet, and the servant, coming in a few minutes later, gathered up all for the ragbag, the contents of which were sold that very afternoon.

"Alas! the worthy ragman had a wife, who, with the curiosity natural to her sex, went through that ragbag. You can imagine the result. Before two days had passed the town was ringing with the scandal. The 'Is it possibles?' and 'I told you sos' were upon every lip. You can fancy the feelings of the poor victims.

"Now, papa, you must give me back my promise, while I make a solemn vow never, never to keep a journal.

"I wonder how much longer I am to stay alone. They have taken Kitty away to punish me, but I am sure it is as much of a punishment for her as it is for me. Thus, you see, the good suffer for the evil deeds of the wicked. I shall now proceed to write that note of apology.

"Your naughty, but unrepentant,

"TEDDY."

CHAPTER IV.

"WELL, old fellow! what success? Got your labor for your pains, eh? I told you so," said Joe Highgate to Jack Fenton on his return from his visit to Ethel.

"By Jove, Joe! I've a good mind to set fire to the old shebang, and rescue the girls," said Jack; "the way they treat those poor little nuns is an outrage on decency. I wonder Ethel Townsend bears it. But you would have lost your bet, old man, for I did see her, although I was told I could n't. She rushed by that old dragon of a Carpenter like a whirlwind. Heavens! how her eyes blazed! I tell you, Joe, she's a trump."

"I say," drawled Joe, "an idea strikes me."

"Well, what is it?" queried Jack. "Let us have it within a week. When an idea strikes you, it generally knocks you senseless."

"It does, eh?" answered Joe, in his slowest way. "Perhaps you had better wait until I recover."

"When you will probably forget all about it."

"Never you mind, my boy," answered Joe, good-naturedly. "Just you get the fellows together this evening. I am going to town now." Said "fellows" being half a dozen sophomores, as full of *diablerie* as themselves.

The next Saturday, as the young ladies were being marshaled along in the usual fashion, they saw in the distance what seemed to be a funeral procession coming toward them. As it came nearer, however, they saw that it was a party of young men, all dressed in solemn black, and marching along in exact imitation of themselves. At the head walked Jack Fenton, and at the foot Joe Highgate, as keepers, bending upon the others an anxious, I-can't-trust-you-a-minute look. No one of the students raised his eyes for a moment from the ground, or gave the smallest sign that they were aware of the presence of the young ladies. It was irresistibly comical, so intensely funny that no one could help laughing. The girls struggled for a moment to restrain their giggles, then burst tumultuously into convulsive fits of laughter. The corners of Miss Eliza's mouth twitched, but whether from anger or amusement, they could not determine. Miss Carpenter was adamant. The girls lost all control over themselves, and, after trying in vain to restore their minds to anything like a serious, contemplative enjoyment of the beauties of nature, Miss Carpenter decided to return to the house. But the young men had not yet finished their wild prank.

"Here, you little Zaccheus," said Joe High-gate to Charlie Adams, the smallest of their number, "shinny up that tree, will you? and see when the little dears turn, and we'll meet 'em again."

The second meeting was even more of a trial for the girls than the first, but they finally reached home and congregated in the young ladies' parlor, while Miss Carpenter, with her face aflame, and the corners of her mouth drawn down in the most uncompromising way, went to seek Madam Leonard.

"Oh, what a lark!" said Lizzie Highgate. This remark was greeted with a shout of laughter, followed by a chorus of voices.

"Wasn't it good! Three cheers for the sophs.!" etc.

"It was the best thing I ever heard of," said Ethel, "and if Miss Carpenter wasn't made of stone throughout, she couldn't have looked so much like a statue through it all. And poor Miss Eliza! how she wanted to laugh! Didn't you pity the poor thing? Oh! it was too good; I tell you, girls, those boys ought to be rewarded for their cleverness. I don't believe that girls, even, could have done better."

"Oh, yes!" cried all in a breath. "Let's show them that we can appreciate a good thing when we see it ; what shall we do ?"

"Wait until after our lecture, for you may be sure that we shall be blamed in some way for this," said Ethel, "and then we will see."

"I am sure," said Edith Preble, "that if Miss Carpenter would use a little common sense, and not force us to appear so ridiculous, the young men would never have thought of this."

Although prepared for the long lecture which came, as was anticipated, Ethel was very indignant, for she knew that it was very unjust in Miss Carpenter to even hint of blame as far they were concerned, and without allowing herself time to think, or to consult with the girls, she seized her pen as soon as she reached her room and wrote to "Jack Fenton and Friends," as follows :—

"GENTLEMEN, — Your motives are understood. We are no longer the simple-minded maidens of this morning. During a lecture this evening on the wickedness of young men in general, and the total depravity of college young men in particular, we were told that you are 'roaring lions going about seeking whom you may devour,' though to tell the truth you did look like the meekest and mildest of lambs, but that was, of course, all outside appearance. Therefore, it was decreed that, on Saturday next, we turn to the sunny left, and leave our beloved woods to you. Hoping that you will no longer disturb our quiet peacefulness, we remain,

"Your natural enemies,

"THE YOUNG LADIES OF MADAM LEONARD'S."

The result was what might have been expected. They had scarcely walked a quarter of a mile the Saturday following, when, seeing the same slow procession of the Saturday before advancing, Miss Carpenter suddenly wheeled her charges, and with undignified haste led them back to the house, saying, —

"Now, young ladies, we will have no more promenades until the proprieties can be observed."

This was what Ethel had not bargained for. She did not like to give up the Saturday promenade, although it was made disagreeable by the presence of her tormentors; besides, she felt not a little ashamed of her part in the proceedings. There was a good deal of talk among the girls, but she preserved a discreet silence. Finally, after thinking the matter over for a few days, she wrote the following letter to Jack Fenton : —

"DEAR JACK, — We were so delighted with the first act of your performance that with one mind and one voice we cried *encore*. That enthusiasm has cost us dear. The strictest watch is kept over us, and we are pining for our accustomed walk. We are forced to take our exercise in the gymnasium and within the grounds. I am sure you will wish to know that we shall not be permitted to go beyond them until Miss Carpenter is quite sure that we shall not again encounter 'the roaring lions' from yonder menagerie. Do not answer this, for we are not allowed to receive letters without previous examination by Madam Leonard, except from our parents. I get this to you through Dumps.   E. T."

Jack Fenton comprehended the situation, and at once set about making arrangements to offer the *amende honorable.* After consulting his comrades he wrote as follows : —

"DEAR MADAM LEONARD, — Regretting our thoughtless joke, and fearing that it may have led to unpleasant consequences for innocent persons, we beg leave to offer our most humble apologies, and to pledge our word of honor that, so far as we are concerned, nothing of the kind shall occur again. Hoping that you will pardon us, we are, with the highest consideration,

> "Your friends,
>> "THE STUDENTS."

No further allusion was ever made to the subject at Madam Leonard's, and everything went on as usual until the day before Thanksgiving, when the girls living near went home for a short vacation.

CHAPTER V.

KITTY and Ethel were in the wildest possible spirits when they reached the Brewster mansion, which was ablaze with light and fragrant with flowers. Kitty rushed into her mother's arms, saying, —

"You dear, blessed old mamma, do you know how glad I am?"

"Yes, dear," answered Mrs. Brewster, smiling, "and I am sure you know how glad we are, too." Then turning to Ethel she kissed her on both cheeks, saying, —

"My dear child, nothing would please us more than to have you consider yourself Kitty's sister while you are here. Pray, make yourself as thoroughly at home as possible."

There was a sudden rush of tears to Ethel's brown eyes at this warm greeting. She could only look her thanks, but she felt sure that Mrs. Brewster understood how grateful she was. Then Mr. Brewster came in, saying, —

"Well, Kittikin, you look as though you had begun to give thanks already."

"Oh, yes, papa, we began the instant we left Madam Leonard's."

He welcomed Ethel very cordially, and she felt at her ease at once. Mr. Brewster, although a thorough man of business, was a delightful host, cordial and sympathetic, with a smile and a kind word for all. He was a tall, handsome man, with dark, piercing eyes, and hair plentifully sprinkled with gray.

"Now, my dears," said Mrs. Brewster, "run upstairs and dress for dinner."

"But where is Margaret?" asked Kitty.

"She is in her room," answered her mother. "She arrived only an hour ago, and feeling rather tired with her journey, I persuaded her to lie down. You will see her soon. Take Ethel to Margaret's old room, and make yourselves presentable. Your trunks have gone up. Shall I send Mary to you?"

"Oh! no," answered Kitty, "we are independent of Marys, are n't we, Ethel?"

"Yes, indeed," she answered, "among other good things we have learned to wait on ourselves, and I think we rather like it."

Kitty led the way to her own room first, and as Ethel caught a glimpse of its dainty furnishings of pink and blue she was in ecstasies.

"Oh! how lovely it is," she exclaimed. "How dreadful Madam Leonard's must seem to you."

"It is my discipline, my dear," said Kitty, philosophically. "I appreciate it all the more when I am permitted to enjoy it. But this is your room, next to mine; it used to be Margaret's. How do you like it? The yellow hangings just suit your hair."

"It is simply perfect," answered Ethel, "and those yellow roses — what a profusion of them!"

"Yes," answered Kitty, "if there is any one thing that mamma fairly dotes upon, it is flowers. They are sent in twice a week from our country-place, a few miles out."

Ethel was soon arrayed in a dark-green silk trimmed with plush of the same shade, with a dainty bit of lace at the throat and a cluster of the yellow roses.

"What a picture you are, and how quickly you dress. I shall wear something you have never seen. How do you like it?" asked Kitty, as she threw on a lovely fawn-colored cashmere trimmed with fans of cardinal silk.

"It is charming," said Ethel, "and it just suits you. How beautifully it lights up."

"Now I must have some flowers to match my trimming," said Kitty, as she rang the bell and ordered some Jacqueminots for her corsage.

"How do you know there are any?" asked Ethel.

"Oh, there are sure to be some, for they are mamma's favorites. She is very particular about the flowers."

Just then Mary returned with the flowers, and after fastening them in their proper places, the two girls descended. Mrs. Onslow met them at the foot of the stairs. She was Kitty's only sister, and was a lovely woman, with a pure, fair, young face, her head crowned with beautiful, abundant, though prematurely gray hair. This crown of glory was the wonder and admiration of her friends. She looked like a picture of some famous court beauty. Kitty was very proud of her, and she looked

for the admiration in Ethel's eyes she was sure
to find there. Peeping shyly from behind her
mamma, "a lesser transcript of herself," was
little five-year-old Gertrude, shaking down her
heavy, dark hair until her face was fairly
covered.

"Oh, you little nun, put back that black
veil!" exclaimed Kitty, trying to catch her
as she ran, with a laugh as sweet and soft as
the trill of a bird, toward the drawing-room.

What a happy evening it was! It was nearly
midnight when they said good-night, Kitty
saying to Ethel : —

"I wonder how it will seem to be allowed
to finish our morning nap? I shall not stir
until half-past eight, and you must not either."

"I shall obey that command without a mur-
mur," answered Ethel with the last good-night.

"Have you provided for your poor pets?"
asked Kitty of her mamma the next morning.

"Oh, yes!" answered Mrs. Brewster.
"They will all have a good dinner to-day."

"I believe that mamma feeds more beggars,"
said Kitty, "than any other person in Boston."

"That's a broad statement, my dear," said

her mother. "I do try to do some good to my fellow-beings, but I do not give indiscriminately; I make a personal investigation in every case, and I am sure that those to whom I give are worthy."

"I should think that that would often be very unpleasant," said Ethel.

"Duty is none the less duty because it is unpleasant, my dear," answered Mrs. Brewster, smiling. "I should feel as though I were shifting my responsibility to other shoulders, if I did not visit my poor myself—besides it is not all unpleasant. There are many sunshiny spots in the dwellings of the poor. Their gratitude is often worth more to me than the trouble I take for them, and they set an example of patience, sometimes, that it would be well for more fortunate ones to imitate. But now with regard to yourselves; what will you do to-day?"

"For my part," answered Ethel, "I should like to just stay here quietly, and enjoy my freedom in this lovely house."

"So you shall, my dear," answered Kitty. "And after luncheon, if you like, we will take a little drive about the city."

"That will suit me exactly," answered Ethel, "for I have not seen Boston since I was a little girl; but for the present, I shall just feast my eyes on these lovely adornments," looking about the charmingly attractive drawing-room.

Mrs. Brewster was a lady of exquisite taste, passionately fond of flowers, and very skilful in arranging them. They met the eye at every turn. There were large pots and lovely jars of growing plants, blossoming profusely, in hall and reception-room, and exquisite vases of cut flowers in library and drawing-room.

She had a pretty fancy of ornamenting the breakfast-table with a glass vase filled with cool-looking, graceful ferns, which were very refreshing to look at. Her house was filled with fine painting, statuary, and other works of art. Wealth and good taste had combined to make it one of the most attractive houses in Boston. It was fortunate for Ethel, stranger as she was, that she should have fallen in with the Brewsters, — true representative Bostonians, — thus enabling her to see Boston as it really is.

"You will have callers to-day, young ladies,"

said Mrs. Brewster, a few hours later, "for everybody knows you are here, and Ethel may expect her papa's old friend, Mr. Apthorpe, who is very desirous of seeing her. I saw him yesterday, and told him you were to be here."

"Oh, I shall be so glad to see somebody who knew papa when he was young!" said Ethel. "He is very fond of Mr. Apthorpe, and has told me so much about him, that I feel as though I knew him well. He is not married, I believe."

"No," answered Mrs. Brewster, "his widowed sister, Mrs. Amesbury, keeps his house, and is a very lovely woman. They proposed taking you away at once."

"Well, that was a cool proposition," said Kitty. "I should like to see them do it. She should n't go away from me, even if she wanted to; she belongs here!"

"Don't be so impetuous, Kitten," said Mrs. Brewster, smiling.

"She is only 'making believe,' dear Mrs. Brewster," said Ethel. "She knows perfectly well that wild horses, even, could n't drag me away from this lovely home."

Just then a young lady was ushered into their presence. Ethel felt that she brought a breeze from the outside world with her. She greeted Kitty effusively, and was then introduced to Ethel as Kitty's friend, Miss Cleveland.

Nana Cleveland was a tall, stylish young lady, with a brilliant brunette complexion and handsome dark eyes, rather overdressed, and with very decided opinions, which she seemed not at all afraid to express. She was bright and clever of speech, but so unpleasantly sharp at times that Ethel felt like trying to suppress her.

"I came, Miss Townsend," she said, "to offer my congratulations for this outing. I was formerly a pupil at Madam Leonard's, and not a favorite pupil, either. By the way," turning to Kitty, "who is the favorite, now that the peerless Julia is no longer there?"

"Lizzie Highgate, I think," answered Kitty. "Do you know her?"

"Little wasp!" said Miss Cleveland, laughing; "I think I do. But do you know why she should be a favorite?"

"It cannot be on account of her agreeable manners," said Kitty.

"I should think not," answered Miss Cleveland. "She was there my last year, and I found her out. It is because she tells madam everything that happens among the girls, barring her own tricks."

"She couldn't be so mean!" exclaimed Ethel, indignantly.

"If you think Miss Highgate overburdened with a sense of honor, Miss Townsend, it shows that you don't know her; but you will be likely to become acquainted with her before the year is out," said Miss Cleveland. "But what are you going to do with yourselves?"

"They will rest to-day," answered Mrs. Brewster, "and then prepare for a quiet little dancing-party which I propose to give for them to-morrow night."

"Oh, mamma!" broke in Kitty; "you are a jewel of the first water. My feet are fairly aching to dance; and see! Ethel's eyes are dancing already. I really cannot keep still," she went on, jumping up and executing a little *pirouette.*

"Oh, Mrs. Brewster!" said Miss Cleveland, noticing that lady's look of disapproval; "do let the poor things enjoy their holiday. Think of the tortures in store for them on their return."

"You should say discipline, Nana," said Mrs. Brewster. "I am sure Kitty shows a lack of it this morning. I am afraid that Madam Leonard is scarcely strict enough."

There was an indignant exclamation from Kitty, while Nana said :—

"She must have changed wonderfully since my last year if that is true. Kitty has my full sympathy. But I want to hear all about it," turning to that young lady; "you girls must spend a day with me before you go back. Shall it be Saturday? I suppose you return to your cells on Monday?"

"I cannot spare them to you this time, Nana," said Mrs. Brewster, answering for them. "Mr. Apthorpe has begged for Ethel without avail, and he has some claim upon her, being one of her papa's oldest friends."

"Oh! do you know that dear, delightful old roaring lion, Miss Townsend? He will probably show you his amiable side, though I confess he often shows the other to me."

"I saw him once," answered Ethel; "but I remember very little of him. Papa is very fond of talking of him. He is very clever, is he not?"

"Clever does not express it at all," answered Miss Cleveland. "He is a wonderful man, my dear: very talented, a great wit, and perfectly at home with every subject, but dreadfully self-opinionated. He won't allow himself to be contradicted; and when you see him shake his mane, look out for a roar."

"You terrify me, Miss Cleveland," said Ethel; "I am not very courageous, and you make me dread to meet him."

"Oh! as to that," she answered, "I predict that you will be one of the favored few, and to be in favor with Mr. Apthorpe is to be considered a very lucky person. You will be pronounced a beauty, or a very clever girl, and perhaps both, at once, for Mr. Apthorpe never notices a woman unless she has, at least, one of these qualifications."

Ethel decided that she didn't like Miss Cleveland at all, and Mrs. Brewster thought it high time to interfere.

"My dear," she said, turning to Nana, "you are talking supreme nonsense. Mr. Apthorpe certainly appreciates a clever woman, and he looks upon a pretty one as he would upon a lovely picture ; only, unfortunately, he often finds that the canvas possesses quite as much soul as the flesh and blood."

"Oh! please, Mrs. Brewster," said Miss Cleveland, with mock humility, "don't crush me any more. Let me up, and I'll be good."

"Oh, well, Miss Nana, you deserved to be crushed," said Mrs. Brewster: "you were trying to give Ethel a false impression."

"I was only trying to put her on her guard," protested Miss Cleveland, "so that she need not walk directly into the lion's mouth, that was all. It is quite a pity, Miss Townsend," she went on, turning to Ethel, "that the charming Gerald is abroad. He is not expected until Christmas."

"And who is 'the charming Gerald,' Miss Cleveland? You forget that I am a stranger," said Ethel.

"You don't mean to say," said Miss Cleveland, holding up her hands in astonishment, "that you have never heard of Major Apthorpe ? Tell her about His Elegance, Mrs. Brewster — words fail me."

Mrs. Brewster shook her finger warningly at Nana, as she answered : —

"He is Mr. Apthorpe's youngest and favorite brother, and, for a gentleman of elegant leisure, is the busiest man I know. He is in great demand socially, being a ready, graceful speaker, and perfectly *au fait* in all matters of etiquette."

"You are to understand, Miss Townsend," said Nana, in a mocking tone, "that Boston would not be Boston without Major Apthorpe. He is the social axle on which the Hub turns."

They all laughed at this retort, while Mrs. Brewster answered, quietly : —

"I am sure the Hub appreciates him, and I, for one, am proud of such a representative. I know of no family who could have entertained 'our late distinguished visitors' as gracefully as the Apthorpes. The major does not spend his time and talents in mere amusements, but he takes the keenest interest in those less favored than himself."

"Cats and dogs, for instance," interrupted Nana.

"Oh, no!" broke in Kitty, who had not spoken before since the last subject was introduced; "they say he hates cats and women: women because they are like cats, and cats because they are like women."

"Oh, Kittikin, Kittikin!" exclaimed Mrs. Brewster. "I shall certainly have to send you to the nursery." Then turning to Ethel, she said:—

"Major Apthorpe is a true gentleman. He is quite as kind and thoughtful in his attentions to older people as to the most petted society belle, and true gentleness is a rare quality nowadays; and if I needed any assistance in my charitable work I should apply to him sooner than to any other man."

"Oh! as to that," said Nana, "I don't deny that he is charitable, in that sense; and I will acknowledge that he is polite, and can pick up and restore a lady's fan with the most perfect grace, and at the same time make her feel that he considers that it was artfully dropped."

"Are you in the habit of dropping your fan,

Miss Nana?" asked Mrs. Brewster, in a provoking tone.

"If I am I was never unfortunate enough to have it returned by His Elegance," retorted Miss Cleveland. "Seriously, what I particularly object to in this thoroughly *blasé* young man is his manner of showing people how gracefully he can endure being bored. One perfectly understands that he has seen everything worth seeing, heard everything worth hearing, and knows everything worth knowing. How I hate that air of fine disdain which has become habitual. I know of no more exasperating mortal living than Major Gerald Apthorpe. He is perfectly insufferable. But, dear me! what a waste of time, when I had so many things to say! I hope, Miss Townsend, that you have been sufficiently warned against falling in love with our much-talked-of young man when you shall see him. Snub him gently but firmly, my dear, and who knows but what he may be piqued into falling in love himself. He would experience a new sensation, I fancy. Now I must really go, but I shall see you again."

As she rose Mrs. Brewster said:—

"I hope we shall see you at our little party."

"Oh! are you really going to be so good as to let me come after abusing your paragon so?" asked Nana.

"You don't deserve it," said Mrs. Brewster, laughing; "but I shall forgive you this time, hoping for better things in future."

Many others called during the morning, and after luncheon the two girls, with little Gertrude, went for a drive. When they returned, two hours later, Mrs. Brewster met them at the door, saying to Ethel, regretfully: —

"I am sorry to tell you, my dear, that you have missed seeing Mr. Apthorpe and Mrs. Amesbury. They seemed disappointed in not finding you; but I promised to take you there to-morrow morning."

"I am sorry to have missed them," said Ethel; "but I cannot tell you how much I dread meeting Mr. Apthorpe. I was looking forward to it with a good deal of pleasure: but Miss Cleveland has spoiled it all."

"Oh! you mustn't mind what Nana says," answered Mrs. Brewster. "The Apthorpes do not appreciate her as she thinks she deserves, and she feels it keenly. There is a want of refinement about her, a brusqueness of manner and speech, that is not pleasing. She was a very precocious child, and she has been flattered injudiciously."

"I am sure she seems to be popular," said Kitty.

"Yes," answered Mrs. Brewster; "she generally has a small court about her, for men like to hear her talk: but they are a little afraid of her sharp speeches. She is too audacious."

"I cannot understand why she should be," said Kitty, "for Mrs. Cleveland is gentleness itself."

"Yes," said her mamma; "and she is an invalid, too, you know; but such traces of poor blood can generally be accounted for, if one goes back far enough."

" Mamma is a thorough aristocrat, you see," said Kitty, laughing, as the two girls went upstairs to lay aside their wraps; "but she has such a dear, kind, charitable heart that very few people suspect it."

"Oh, Kitty," said Ethel, the next morning, as she was dressing for the much-dreaded visit,

"do tell me what to wear. I feel as though I
were going to be put on exhibition."

"Go just as you are! Miss Flora McFlimsy.
Why do you ask me? you are always lovely."

"Go to! flatterer," answered Ethel. "It is
of no earthly use to ask you: you are prejudiced. I'll wear the plainest thing I have."

Ethel knew how to dress. Her toilettes
were always harmonious, and when she pre-
sented herself before Mrs. Brewster, as she
laughingly said, "for criticism," that lady was
delighted. She wore a black velvet costume,
which fitted her graceful form perfectly, and a
Gainsborough hat, which set off her lovely face
and brought out its beauty. The only color
about her was a cluster of yellow roses fastened
below the throat, a little to the left.

"My dear," said Mrs. Brewster, who felt
that she needed encouragement, "you are
bewitching. You have set out to captivate
Richard Apthorpe and you will do it. I am
sure of it."   ·

"Oh! Mrs. Brewster," said Ethel, well
pleased, "do you really think I look well? I am
so anxious to do my papa's daughter justice."

"Never fear for your papa's daughter, my dear: I am very proud of her."

. . . .

"My DEAR PAPA, — This is Sunday, the last day of my visit at the Brewsters', which has been thoroughly delightful. On Friday evening Mrs. Brewster gave a small dancing-party. She was kind enough to ask Jack Fenton on my account, and was so pleased with him that she invited him to come whenever he liked. Was not that good of her? But no one could help liking Jack. He told me that he was going into the country to spend Sunday with one of his chums. So I did not see him again. I am very proud of Jack. His manners are perfect and he dances divinely. I could see that the young ladies were quite impressed by him, and it is not to be wondered at. He seemed greatly superior to the other young men present, some of whom were very young. They all danced well, but they did not seem to have any ideas, or if they did, they did not know how to express them. They were all alike in this respect. There was absolutely no conversation, except between Jack and Miss

Nana Cleveland. This young lady was a former pupil of Madam Leonard's, and is a friend
of Kitty's. She is very bright and amusing,
and, while I do not wholly admire her, I like
to hear her talk.

"We see now the blessed result of what
Kitty calls our discipline. We enjoy everything
with so much more zest than we otherwise
could. I have not had a moment's time to
write before since I came, but I have saved up
everything until now, and shall tell you of all
our good times. (I am afraid I am getting
Yankeefied.)

"Why! papa, dear, we have been almost
beside ourselves with happiness. And do you
know what a dear, delightful place Boston is?
Of course, you do, in a degree, but it has
changed since you knew it. How many times
I have wished you were here since I came for
this little visit. Such lovely drives! and such
charming people! I called at Mr. Apthorpe's
on Friday. I started with fear and trembling,
and came away enchanted. What a thoroughly
charming man he is! He said a great many
pleasant things of you. He noticed that I

have your eyes and the same firm mouth. You always said that I had a wilful mouth, so it seems that the same mouth can be firm in one person and wilful in another. How is that? I should like a little explanation, if you please. Mrs. Amesbury was very sweet and cordial, and invited me to spend the Christmas holidays with them.

"'Of course she will!' said Mr. Apthorpe. 'I should like to know who has a better right to Ned Townsend's daughter than I.' 'You will find it hard to make your peace with Kitty if you take Ethel from us,' said Mrs. Brewster. 'You must teach Miss Kitty not to be selfish,' said Mr. Apthorpe.

"They are the best of friends, and Mrs. Brewster admires him immensely. Indeed, no one could help it. You will be glad to know that I have promised them a large part of the Christmas holidays. The only drawback to my delightful anticipations is the fact that Major Apthorpe will be here. Why have you not told me of the existence of this important gentleman. So important, first of all to himself, according to Miss Cleveland, so important

to his friends, and so important to Boston.
Mrs. Amesbury talked of him constantly. It
was 'Gerald, Gerald,' during my entire call,
with now and then a 'Jed' from Mr. Apthorpe.
Evidently they have tried to spoil him, and
have succeeded admirably, but I hate conceited
people, and I am wicked enough to hope that
something will happen to keep him on the
other side until after the holidays.

"Papa, dear, if you should, by any means, get
hold of him, on no account let him go. Now,
am I not showing a very unamiable disposition
when everybody is so kind to me? You must
be ashamed of me, and, to tell the truth, I am
ashamed of myself. All the same, I hope he
will not come, notwithstanding Kitty privately
assures me that he is really uncommonly nice.

"I want you to know Kitty's sister, Mrs.
Onslow. She is the loveliest woman I ever
saw, but she is very delicate in health. Kitty
and I are to visit her in the summer. Mr.
Onslow is very proud of his wife, but his mind
is unreasonably full of business. He seems
always in a hurry. I look upon him in amazement. He seems to have absolutely no

leisure, and I find myself wondering how long he will live in this way. All this seems very strange to me. I have been so accustomed to men of leisure, all my life, that I cannot understand how any man can live in the midst of excitement all the time, and keep his mental balance; but nobody else seems to mind it.

"Mr. Brewster is a busy man, too, but as he leaves business behind him when he comes home, he is able to rest. I think Mr. Onslow must carry on business even in his sleep.

"To-morrow we go back to Madam Leonard's, but I go with the lightest possible heart, having such delightful anticipations. I shall live upon them until they are realized.

"We went to St. Paul's this morning. The rector preached a very eloquent sermon; I am sure you would have appreciated it. He is so much in earnest himself that it is impossible that his hearers should not be in earnest, too. No one could be drowsy under his preaching. And it is such a fine place in which to take a nap, too! Such a lovely, curious old church, with high boxes for pews. I am ashamed to say that I was very much amused, during the service, to watch a little old lady in front of me, whose head I could scarcely see when she was sitting. It was so comical to see her pop up like a Jack-in-the-box, every little while, but the doctor's voice was so impressive that I felt rebuked and very soon ceased to think of my surroundings. The rector impresses me as a man to be wholly loved for his goodness and wholly admired for his eloquence.

"Papa, dear, why do you not write a book? I fancied myself with you while reading your last letter. Your descriptions are so charmingly vivid that it seems almost wicked not to allow the world to enjoy them. I am going to whisper a secret. It is my pet ambition to write a book. After I get through with my studies I mean to go away somewhere and shut myself up, and write a wonderful book about the people I have met. I shall call it 'Stories of Peculiar People.' It will be a strange book, unlike any other, if I write it truthfully, as I mean to. Oh, you need not smile, for I certainly mean to do it.

"I must not forget to tell you that I visited

Thatcher (he is the Worth of Boston), on
Friday, and had a glimpse of Paris. You have
thought me too economical, but when I tell you
what I am to pay for one of Thatcher's crea-
tions, the loveliest of walking-costumes, you
will perhaps change your mind. Kitty says
one glance of his artistic eye, which takes in
your general style, costs fifty dollars — but that
is a mere trifle. Such things as linings, facings,
silk, and twist, the magnificent Thatcher takes
no note of, but the bill for the completed
costume makes you think you have a double
vision. But his gowns are marvelous, as to fit
and style, and leave nothing to be desired. I
am to have an evening-dress of pale yellow,
for little dancing-parties such as Mrs. Brewster
often gives. Kitty is to have a pink one. And,
papa, dear, please send me quantities of the
palest amber you can find for my neck, arms,
and dear little ears, and I will kiss you a
thousand times.   Your loving

" TEDDY."

"P. S. — Kitty came in and forced me to
leave off before I had quite finished, and I
came back to say that we are going to be good,

Oh! very good, indeed, Kitty and I, better
even than Miss Edith Preble, who is always
good and proper. And, papa, I want to give
you just the tiniest bit of a hint. While you
are buying my amber, I want you to remember
that pink is very becoming to Kitty, and that,
as I told you, she is to have a pink gown, and I
am sure that a lovely set of pale pink coral
would be exactly what would please her most.

"TED."

CHAPTER VI.

THE WIDOW WYSE.

PRETTY, fair Mrs. Houlton sat in her sunshiny morning-room, industriously darning one
of her own well-worn stockings. By her side,
upon the floor, was a convenient basket,
trimmed with wine-colored velvet handsomely
embroidered. Upon the table near were the
most popular magazines, the latest novel, a few
books celebrated for their intellectual worth,
and a copy of Browning's poems, all of which,
if we except the first-mentioned books, entirely
above the little woman's comprehension. But,
as she had often said to her daughter, "One
must be in the fashion, my dear," and it was
beginning to be the fashion, even in Alliance,
to have literary tastes and aspirations.

Being the widow of the famous (in his little
town) Judge Houlton, she felt that considerable
homage was due her, consequently she carried
herself very proudly before her less fortunate
neighbors; but, unfortunately for her pride,

she was left with a very small income, nobody
knew how small, for she had the "faculty," as
they say in New England, of making a little go
a great way. She was smiling softly to herself,
for she was thinking that in a few weeks her
clever daughter, whom she had not seen in two
years, would be with her, and would bring her
at least one new gown — of which she was
sadly in need — and the latest Paris fashions.
A letter to that effect had reached her that
morning, much to her joy, for she had not
expected her for some months.

Mrs. Houlton was carefully and youthfully
dressed, from the little square of *crêpe lisse*
which did duty as a widow's cap, to the jet
buckles on her slippers; and with her crimped
hair brought low on her white forehead, was still
young looking. She had been no companion
for her husband. She was but a pet and play-
thing in their early married life; but she
disappointed him sorely, and after a time she
used to say to her children, "He cares for
nothing but his books; we must not disturb
him," and very considerately left him alone;
and when at last he died, she took what her

daughter called a sensible and philosophic view
of the matter. She knew that grief and tears
inevitably brought dimness to the eyes and
wrinkles to the forehead; so, after six month's
retirement behind folds upon folds of *crêpe*,
with her natural gayety a little subdued, and
her sombreness lightened by bands of jet, she
showed herself to the world, a beautiful spirit
of resignation.

There was one peculiarity about this mother
and daughter that I must speak of here. They
never allowed themselves to be surprised.
The doorbell, for instance, was hung so that
it could be heard throughout the house. She
had received long letters from her beloved
Julia (and her powers of invention were
marvelous), and yet no one came. She was
longing to tell some gossiping neighbor of
the social successes of her favorite daughter, —
Annie, the elder, had married a poor store-
keeper against her mamma's judgment, and
so did n't signify, — when she heard the welcome sound of the doorbell.

Without the slightest sign of disturbance
or flutter, Mrs. Houlton quietly dropped the

stocking she had been darning into the convenient basket, and pushed it with her foot
farther under the table, while from its dainty
receptacle on the table she took a delicate
piece of embroidery, which she carelessly
dropped in her lap. Then she reached for the
volume of Browning, and she was prepared for
anybody.

"Dear Mrs. Houlton!" said her visitor, the
wife of one of her late husband's young friends,
as she fluttered in, "how charmingly cool and
comfortable you look! I have been in a perfect fever all the morning; and what with poor
servants and fretful children, I had almost made
up my mind that life was *not* worth living,
when I thought of you. I knew I should find
you just as you are, with your book and
embroidery. How you ever find time for so
much reading and fancy-work I cannot understand. And everything seems to run so
smoothly in your house, too. Your servants
are so perfectly trained, and you never seem
to be in a flutter. Do tell me how it is done.
I am in despair."

Mrs. Houlton had, in anticipation of her

daughter's return, engaged old Hannah's niece, so she could truthfully say "my servants," which she did with the smile of a superior.

"I *require* my servants to do their duty. You see, my dear, I don't *expect* anything else, and they know it. The only way to get along comfortably is to let your servants understand, to begin with, that you are mistress of your own house."

The truth is, Mrs. Houlton had had the same old servant for years, who ruled the household with a rod of iron. Her mistress would not have dared to say her soul was her own even, much less her kitchen. She was one of those rare old creatures who, dreading change, accept low wages for a home, and take a personal interest in the family they serve. She was fond of Mrs. Houlton, in her peculiar way, and proud of Miss Julia, as she still called her; but when she said, after a timid suggestion from her mistress, "La! Mrs. Houlton, you don't want that," it amounted to a command.

"I know you are right," answered her guest, "but I give up to my servants, and I cannot help it. They rule me instead of my ruling them."

"You must not let them, my dear ; you must assert yourself," said Mrs. Houlton.

"Ah! it is easy for you to do it, but not for me," said poor Mrs. Adams, with a sigh. Then, spying the basket under the table, she exclaimed : —

"Oh! what lovely embroidery! Did you do it?"

"Do you like it?" said Mrs. Houlton, carelessly ; "it is rather pretty, I think." She did not explain that it was a foreign production, sent by her daughter. It was not necessary. But she went on to say : —

"I am very fond of embroidery. It is a recreation. I do a little every day, because I enjoy it ; and if I did not try to improve my mind a little every day, also, I should consider the day misspent," looking affectionately at the copy of Browning in her hand.

"And you read Browning, too?" said little Mrs. Adams. "I never think of touching his poems ; they are wholly incomprehensible."

"Do you think so?" asked Mrs. Houlton, with a pitying smile. "I am afraid you do not like real poetry, my dear."

"I don't like anything I don't understand," said Mrs. Adams, candidly. "But, dear Mrs. Houlton, you are expecting your charming daughter soon, I hear. How happy you must be, and proud, too! Everybody is on the tiptoe of expectation. She is such a stylish creature, she will be more admired than ever. Such an acquisition as she will be! I do hope she comes to stay!"

"I am her mother," said Mrs. Houlton, with a satisfied smile, "and may be excused for taking pleasure in hearing her praises. Julia has pleasing manners and is generally a success wherever she goes. She was always a favorite among the girls, and I hear from others: she herself is very reticent : that she is very much admired abroad." Then followed an interesting account of dear Julia's social successes, and a list of her admirers.

"We must try and make it pleasant for her," said Mrs. Houlton, artfully, as her visitor rose to go, "for this little place must seem very dull to her under any circumstances."

And Mrs. Adams went home impressed with the idea that she and her friends must

exert themselves to the utmost to "make it
pleasant" for Julia Wyse, when she should do
her native place the honor of visiting it again.

The next day toward evening, as Mrs. Houlton was caressing the volume of Browning,
which she never read, there was a bustle outside, a hasty ring mingled with a barking of
dogs, and a bewildering mixture of French and
English. Mrs. Houlton glanced hastily out of
the window. There stood a smart French
maid with two dogs, one in her arms, and
the other dragging by a ribbon, which she
was alternately scolding and petting. In
another moment she was clasping her beloved
Julia in her arms. It was such a great surprise, for she had not expected her for three
weeks at least, that she almost fainted from
excitement.

"You dear, blessed, little mamma," exclaimed her daughter, "how white you are!
So you are really glad to see me? Ninette,"
turning to her maid, "bring a little wine."

Ninette opened a small traveling-bag and
produced the wine, which quite revived Madam
Houlton.

"Now, mamma," said the affectionate daughter, "if you will allow me to go to my room for a while, — I see the luggage has followed us closely, — I shall give you as much of my society as you will wish, after I have rested a little."

"Poor dear!" said Mrs. Houlton, "you must be dreadfully fatigued, although I must say I never saw you looking better."

"Oh! as to that," said Mrs. Wyse, "you know that I never allow myself to get very tired. We had a quick passage, and I was not seasick; besides I stayed a week in New York. I like to present myself to my friends in the best possible light."

"For my part," answered her partial mamma, "I can say that you are wonderfully improved, my dear, and I am glad you rested on the way, although if I had known you were so near I should hardly have remained contented here."

"All of which shows my wisdom in not letting you know," said her daughter as she left the room.

For the next few days Mrs. Wyse's tongue was busy with that inexhaustible subject, herself, before a delighted audience of one, her mamma. Occasionally her commonplace sister, Mrs. Fielding, would steal away from her numerous family cares to listen with unbounded admiration, for an hour, to the vivid pictures of her much-admired sister's foreign life. As she represented it, her traveling was a triumphal march, and she received a constant ovation wherever she stopped. "I don't envy you," said poor Annie Fielding; "I am glad to have you enjoy so much, but I do sometimes wish that I could get away for a little rest and recreation."

"Oh! Annie," said Mrs. Wyse, reproachfully, "how can you want to leave those dear little children? If I had a little girl like your Julia," putting her handkerchief to her eyes, "I should be perfectly happy; I should never want to leave her."

"I suppose I am wicked," said poor, dragged-out Annie, "but it is only when I get very tired that I feel so."

"Poor dear," said Mrs. Wyse, with a sudden feeling of pity at Annie's forlorn appearance, "you do look worn out, but, for mercy's sake!

don't get low-spirited. It would make me ill at once to see you so. Come upstairs and see what I have for that dear, little rosebud, my namesake."

And Annie was cheered by numerous little presents for herself and children, and she went home, saying to herself: "What a tender heart Julia has! She cannot bear to even hear of other peoples' woes, and she is so generous, too. To be sure, she is rich, but the rich people are not always generous, like Julia."

"How easy it is to make her happy," said Mrs. Wyse to her mother as she went out. "And we ought to do something for her, for she does have a hard time. I should die in a week if I had to live as she does, with those dreadful children always clamoring for something."

"Oh, my dear, you could n't bear it, of course," said her mother; "but she is differently constituted. She is quite satisfied, as a general thing, and if she is not, it is her own fault. She chose to marry a poor man against my judgment, as you well know, and she must suffer the consequences. I did not expect her to make a brilliant match, but there was Mr. Tremaine" —

"Oh, mamma," said Julia, "I don't blame her for refusing him. He was so old and so intensely disagreeable " —

"But he is as rich as a Jew," said her mother.

"And a horrid old screw, as Annie said at the time, I remember," said Mrs. Wyse.

"To add another rhyme, it is very, very true," said Mrs. Houlton, laughing; "but we will change the subject, if you please: it is getting disagreeable."

"Very well," said her daughter, " I am more than willing."

They perfectly understood one another, this clever daughter of a not over-scrupulous mother. But the daughter was, by far, the more accomplished woman of the world, and Mrs. Houlton, recognizing this fact, yielded both admiration and will.

"I am dying to know why you came home earlier than you intended," said Mrs. Houlton, a day or two after this; "but knowing that you do not like to be questioned, I have waited for you to tell me."

"My dear mamma," answered her daughter, "you taught me early to find out other peoples' business, but to guard jealously my own, and I have forgotten neither precept nor example. I remember, when I was very young, I used to listen with wonder and amazement to your skilful manner of asking questions, and your guarded way of answering them. I am an apt pupil of a very clever teacher."

"But I am your mother, Julia," said Mrs. Houlton, reproachfully, "and you should have no secrets from me. I am sure I have always been devoted to your interests."

"Very true, mamma," answered Mrs. Wyse, "and when my plans are fully matured you shall know them, for I shall want your assist-ance. Until then you must be patient. I can only tell you now that I go to Boston in two weeks for a short visit to Nana Cleveland, and before I come back I shall call upon that dear old humbug, Madam Leonard."

"But, Julia, you are surely not going to leave me again so soon!" cried her mother; "and I thought you hated Miss Cleveland."

"Softly, dear mamma," said Mrs. Wyse,

laughing ; " I love everybody, even **Nana Cleve-**
land, when she can be useful to me. You
spoke of a reception. I would suggest that you
fix upon next Tuesday evening. It will remind
people of their duty to me in this respect. I
do not expect to be gone long, and I should die
of *ennui* in this poky old place, without some
excitement."

" Frivolous, as you used to be," said Mrs.
Houlton, " but undoubtedly clever."

" I quite agree with you, although some
people have been uncomplimentary enough
to call it shrewdness, and you might also say
successful. They say that 'nothing succeeds
like success,' and I have made it a point never
to fail. It will please you, I am sure, to know
that I am indebted to you for an expression
that I have found wonderfully taking. It is
this : 'How perfectly lovely !' I remember dis-
tinctly that you said, as I was leaving for my
first little party, now Julia be sure you remember to say, when you come away, 'I have had
a *perfectly lovely* time.' It will be very impolite
if you do not, and if they show you anything
to please you, say, 'Oh! how *perfectly lovely.*'

I have used that expression, as Annie's little Julia would say, four hundred million times. It never fails to please. Oh ! yes, flattery costs nothing and is pleasing to everybody."

" And yet I have heard people say that they were proof against it," said Mrs. Houlton.

"And they are the very people that are most susceptible of it," answered her daughter. "There is not a man in the world," she went on, with a little more than her usual energy, "who has not some weak point to assail, that flattery cannot reach, and I believe that intellectual men are weakest of all in this respect. They generally marry simpletons who are willing to offer perpetual adoration. Their vanity is satisfied with nothing else. But to go back to your first remark, I am going to give you a hint, a bare hint," she repeated, seeing that her mother had started up eagerly. "I made the acquaintance of a young man in Germany, who interested me a good deal, and whom, I flatter myself, I interested still more. He intends leaving in the spring for America with his friend, a young American, who went to Germany to finish his studies. A cousin, by

the way, of Miss Cleveland, of Boston. I had
planned to leave about that time, as you know.
I preferred to be followed, rather than follow.
That is all."

"But, Julia"— began Mrs. Houlton.

"Now, mamma," said her daughter, coldly, "I
said you were to have a hint, merely. You
positively must not ask me any questions. I
should not have spoken of the matter at all,
only I want this young man to be cordially
received, should he come here."

"You are the most provoking person living,"
said poor Mrs. Houlton, who was in an agony
of curiosity.

"I know it, mamma," answered Mrs. Wyse,
"and I sympathize with you heartily, but,"
reaching for the bell-rope, "I cannot help
you."

"Madame?" said the soft voice of Ninette,
but soft as it was, it startled Mrs. Houlton,
for she had not heard the still softer step of
her daughter's invaluable French maid.

"Fetch Bijou and Pet," said her mistress.
"I have not seen them to-day."

"Yes, madame," said Ninette, disappearing.

"She must have been near the door, to have answered so soon," said Mrs. Houlton, suspiciously.

"Oh, I dare say she has been listening," said Mrs. Wyse, carelessly. "It is a way these maids have."

"You should not permit it," said Mrs Houlton. "It is very foolish of you."

Mrs. Wyse shrugged her pretty shoulders, but did not answer.

"See, mamma!" she said, a moment later, as she fondled the pretty creatures, which seemed overjoyed to see her. "Kiss me, Bijou. Shake hands, Pet. Ninette, you must show off their accomplishments to mamma. They know a good deal more than a good many human beings."

They went through a good many clever tricks, greatly to the amusement of the two ladies.

"Now you may take them out for a little exercise, Ninette," said her mistress; "but first come to me, you little troublesome comforts, and say good-by."

They gave two soft, quick barks, in answer, as they rushed into her arms.

"Hear them, mamma," she said. "They understand me; and do you see how they love me? I think I love them as well as Annie does her little Julia."

"Ah! how can they help loafing what is so loafly? *les pauvres innocents!*" said Ninette, in low, ecstatic tones.

Mrs. Wyse shook her finger playfully at her maid, saying, —

"Flatterer!"

"Ah! non, madame" —

"You see," said Mrs. Wyse, interrupting her and turning to her mother, "they all spoil me, even Ninette."

"I do really think, Julia," said Mrs. Houlton, indignantly, as that person went out, "that you allow Ninette to be too familiar. I have noticed it a good deal, and I believe that you are making a mistake."

"Poor Ninette!" answered her daughter: "I took her from slavery and she does not forget it. She is perfectly devoted to me — such a faithful creature! Why, I could not get along a day without her! I think you hardly know how much I am indebted to her

for what you are pleased to call 'my improved
personal appearance.' Of course she knows a
good many of my secrets; but she is very wise,
is my little Ninette. I make it worth her
while to be. Oh, yes! never fear. Ninette
is all right. She knows what is for her
interest."

"What a convenience you make of those
dogs, Julia," said Mrs. Houlton, with a little
warmth, as her mind went back to the interrupted subject.

"Oh, yes!" said her daughter, with the
utmost candor; "I send for them when I want
to change a subject, as you notice. I really
don't know what I should do without them.
They amuse me, and they never ask disagreeable questions."

CHAPTER VII

GAYETIES.

Mrs. Houlton's pleasant rooms were crowded with enthusiastic admirers on the evening of the reception. The Widow Wyse wore a gown which every one pronounced the perfection of good taste, and which set off her lovely complexion as nothing else could. It was of a black, gauzy material, through which her perfectly formed arms were seen to the best advantage. The overskirt was looped with clusters of purplish-black pansies, their yellow hearts gleaming like the coils of her tawny hair. It was evident that the Widow Wyse had made up her mind to be irresistible this evening. The fervor with which she said to everybody, "I am *so* glad to get back to the dear old place and the dear old friends," charmed one and all. She talked with the new rector as though her happiness depended upon the welfare of the Church. He was delighted with her quick appreciation, her ready acquiescence in his views, her humble deference to his opinions, her evident interest in the poor of the parish; and her conquest was complete when, after a few words of delicate flattery, she offered to start a bazar for the benefit of "The Church Poor Fund" immediately after her return from Boston; and a few minutes later he startled one of the older parishioners whom he had heard speaking of her as a gay woman of fashion, by saying, —

"She may be called so, but a less worldly minded woman I have seldom met."

He had known her just half an hour. Indeed, they all seemed under a spell. She displayed the most eager interest in the most trifling amusements of the younger portion of society, and they flattered themselves that it was their pleasure that she was seeking to promote, as she told them her plans and projects.

"Dear Mrs. Wyse!" said one enthusiastic young lady, "somebody says that you are going to leave us soon; but you must not. Indeed, we will not let you go. We have so counted on your coming back! It has been as dull as the catacombs, so far this winter. We might as well be mummies, and done with it."

"You dear little rosebud!" said Mrs. Wyse, laughing softly. "Who says such a dreadful thing? Do you think I could stay away long, and leave you to wither in this dull place, especially after such an appeal? Indeed, I am only tearing myself away for a week or two. I shall be only too glad to come back and help you to be merry, for I am" —

And she turned away to speak to a passing friend. The Widow Wyse had a way of turning at a half-finished sentence. She often found it convenient.

"Just the same as ever!" exclaimed the enthusiastic young lady. "So delightfully impulsive! She always had a habit of breaking off in this way."

"Rather an annoying habit, I should say," spoke out a lady who was getting to be called an old maid by the very young ladies in society.

"I think she is perfectly lovely," said the first young lady. "She does n't look a day older than she did when she went away.

What a lovely complexion she has, and what a charming dimple in her left cheek!"

"Yes," answered Miss Brown, the old young lady. "I noticed that dimple, too. It is a new one. She didn't have it when she went away."

"What can you mean?" said the others, in a breath.

"Why," said Miss Brown, "don't you know that they make dimples in Paris? You can have them as deep as you like, only you have to submit to a surgical operation to accomplish it. She has another on her shoulder. I suppose that was an experiment."

"But how do you know anything about it?" queried one of the young ladies.

"Her maid told Mrs. Jaques, the seamstress, who was assisting her on Mrs. Houlton's dress, last week. You know she is a great gossip."

"Yes, she *is* a great gossip, and I don't believe a word she says," said Mrs. Wyse's admirer, with warmth. All the same, the young ladies, as they turned away, puckered their young foreheads in trying to remember whether Mrs. Wyse had dimples when she went abroad.

CHAPTER VIII.

"DEAR, dear, dear me! what a flutter Miss Highgate is in this morning, to be sure," said Kitty one morning just before Christmas, "and madam, too, is scarcely less excited, and all because of a note from the Widow Wyse."

"And what of the Widow Wyse?" said Ethel. "Has she come back to her native land?"

"Not only has she come back," answered Kitty, "but she is to be here to-day, and our history is to be given up in consequence."

"Oh, bless the Widow Wyse!" said Ethel, throwing down her book. "I won't study another word, as it would do no good. I couldn't possibly remember the dates and things until to-morrow, to save my life. Bless the Widow Wyse! I say again. Bless anybody who saves me history. But tell me more about this engaging person. She is wealthy, of course, or Lizzie Highgate wouldn't worship her."

"Oh, yes," answered Kitty, "at least it is supposed so. She married a man considerably more than twice her age for his money, and, as Madam Leonard says, 'She bears her loss very sweetly.'"

"I hope crêpe is becoming to her," said Ethel, laughing.

"Oh, bless you, she does n't wear crêpe," said Kitty. "She says that owing to her delicate organization her physicians have forbidden it. Lustreless black silks and delicate gauzes are becoming to everybody, and mauve ribbons would especially suit the Widow Wyse's fair complexion. She is really pretty, and you must be prepared for a decidedly dashing widow."

"She will find me very amiable, on account of the lesson she has spared me," said Ethel, as they went to a recitation.

In the middle of the afternoon as Kitty was standing by the window, she suddenly exclaimed: "Come, Ethel, quickly, here she is."

"How young she looks," said Ethel. "I expected to see an older person."

"Yes," admitted Kitty, "she does look young from here, younger than she did when

she left school, but a brush of powder and
a *soupçon* of *rouge* will accomplish wonders in
a woman's face sometimes, if she is skilful."

"You dreadful girl," exclaimed Ethel, "you
talk like a 'world-worn cynic,' and an old
bachelor besides. I am ashamed of you. What
would your dear, charitable mother say to you?
Here am I, ready to embrace her."

"I don't hate history as you do," said Kitty,
dryly.

"But — you do hate the Widow Wyse,"
answered Ethel; "anybody can see that."

"No," said Kitty, "I don't think I do, but I
hate to have people make such a fuss over anybody."

"Especially the Widow Wyse," said Ethel.

"Especially the Widow Wyse," admitted
Kitty. .

An hour later they were summoned to the
drawing-room. Mrs. Wyse, moving swiftly
toward Kitty, taking both hands and kissing
her impulsively on both cheeks, said : —

"You dear, little Kitten, I am so glad to see
you, and to see you here. It seems as though
I had hardly been away. I feel like a school-
girl again instead of a" —

Here she broke off, dropped her eyes with a sigh of deep emotion, made an effective pause, winked fast two or three times, then noticing Ethel, as if for the first time, she moved toward her, offering her hand, with a sweet smile:—

"And this, I know, is Miss Townsend. I shall not need a formal introduction, I am sure, when I tell you that I saw your dear papa but a few days before I left Dresden."

"Oh, have you really seen papa recently?" exclaimed Ethel, eagerly. "How was he? He writes me often, but I should like to know if he was looking well and happy when you saw him?"

"He was looking very well. Very proud when speaking of you, my dear, and very handsome. Indeed, they call him 'the handsome American,' in Dresden. I met him first in Paris, and I thought him a little sad, but he was much improved when I saw him last, but he misses you sorely yet, and is looking forward impatiently to the time when he may expect you to join him."

Then turning to Madam Leonard, she said: "How lovely it is here, and how kind of you to permit me to see these dear girls. I could almost beg of you to take me again as a pupil."

"Indeed, I wish I might," said Madam Leonard, fervently.

"And now," said Mrs. Wyse, rising, "I am sorry to say I must go."

"Oh, do not go yet, my dear," said Madam Leonard, earnestly; "you know how glad we should be to keep you with us to-night."

"Don't tempt me, dear madam," said the fair widow. "I must not stay. I promised Nana faithfully that I would be back to-night. It is so hard to refuse such an invitation, but I shall see you again soon."

"How is Nana?" asked Madam Leonard, indifferently.

"Oh, the same as ever," said Mrs. Wyse, with a soft laugh. "She is so bright and keen that I am positively afraid of her. Those flashing retorts are always on the end of her tongue. I told her this morning that I was constantly seeing sparks and trying to dodge them."

"These sarcastic speeches do Miss Cleveland no credit," said Madam Leonard, severely.

"But she is so uncommonly bright," said

Mrs. Wyse. "I often wish I had the gift of making such amazingly witty speeches."

"Don't wish it, my dear," answered madam. "I am sure no one would wish to be so disliked," remembering her former pupil's many pert remarks.

"Oh, no, indeed!" exclaimed the charming Widow Wyse. "I want everybody to love me. I think it would break my heart to know that anybody really disliked me."

"Well," said Kitty, with a rising inflection, when the girls were again by themselves.

"Well," answered Ethel, with a provoking, falling inflection.

"Don't be stupid," said Kitty, impatiently. "What do you think of the Widow Wyse?"

"If I must give an opinion on a five minutes' acquaintance," said Ethel, slowly, "I should say that she seems amiable, and is certainly a pretty, graceful young woman."

"She does seem so," said Kitty, reluctantly. "She is certainly changed since I saw her last. She doesn't look quite the same. She could hardly help improving with the advantages she has had; but there is something about her face that puzzles me. I can't make out what it is."

"She has a youthful face," answered Ethel, "in spite of your objectionable powder, but I should think some of it would get lodged in that deep dimple sometimes."

"That's it," exclaimed Kitty, "it is that dimple that has changed her."

"But she must have had that always," said Ethel.

"She certainly did not have it when she went away," persisted Kitty.

"Oh! you dear, absurd little Kitten!" said Ethel, laughing; "you are so prejudiced against the Widow Wyse that you won't allow her that poor little dimple. For shame!"

"I never was so puzzled in my life," said Kitty, dismissing the subject.

Mrs. Wyse had told her mother that there was one man in Boston that she particularly desired to meet again, and she was fortunate in the fulfilment of this desire. Mr. Apthorpe had overtaken her one morning as she was walking with Nana across the Common. He accosted the latter with —

"Well, Miss Nana, are you taking a walk to sharpen your wits this frosty morning?"

"Yes," she answered, quickly, "and I see that you are doing the same. I hope we shall meet later."

He laughed at her quick answer, as though amused. Then she said to her companion, in the same mocking tone: "Julia, this is my dear friend Mr. Apthorpe, who loves me, even though he often chastises me. Mrs. Wyse — Mr. Apthorpe."

"Ah, Mr. Apthorpe," said the fair widow, in a soft, low voice which contrasted strangely with Nana's, "I did hope to see recognition in your eyes," as she gave him her hand.

"I have met you before. I was sure of it before you spoke, for I seldom forget faces. You must pardon me for forgetting your name."

"Yes," she answered, "in Paris; but I was foolish to expect you to remember me, as we met but once, and only for a short time. Of course I could not forget you; besides, I have been reminded of you so many times by an old friend of yours, Dr. Townsend, of Mobile."

"Ah, Dr. Townsend," said Mr. Apthorpe, interested at once. "So you know him?" And forthwith began to talk of him in a very animated, interesting way as they walked on, until Nana, after trying in vain to get her companion's attention, said : —

" I positively must interrupt you, for we have an important engagement this morning, and you have, by your enchantment, like the Pied Piper of Hamelin, drawn us after you, entirely out of our way."

" I was so glad to meet him again," said Mrs. Wyse, after they had left him almost at his very door.   " Is he not charming ? "

" Very charming, when he chooses to be, which is not always, as I have the misfortune to know," answered Nana.

" How do you dare to answer him as you do sometimes?" asked Mrs. Wyse.

"Oh, I always dare to say anything I choose," said the irrepressible Nana.   " But if you could hear him talk to me sometimes ; nothing that I could say would surprise you.   I assure you, his language is often more forcible than polite."

CHAPTER IX.

COUNTRY GAYETIES.

MRS. WYSE went back to her mamma, after having exacted a promise from Nana to visit her during the month of May, quite well satisfied with her visit. She had accomplished all that she had planned for, and she was in a most amiable frame of mind. She was ready to do her part in the social world of Alliance. She was as good as her word, as far as gayeties were concerned, for she could not live without excitement. Society was an absolute necessity for her. Invitations poured in from all quarters. Balls, theatricals, and other entertainments, followed in quick succession. All this distracting flurry had an exhilarating effect upon her spirits. The young girls went wild over her; but after a while their mothers began to shake their heads, for her spirits sometimes ran away with her. There was a spice of Bohemianism in her gayety, noticeable as she grew more careless of being observed,

that scarcely kept her to the conventionalities
of life; but she had such an appearance of
cheerful good-nature that it was easy to forgive
her sometimes too gay spirits. She had, also,
the rare gift of making people believe that
they were fully appreciated — the inestimable
gift of flattery. Intellectual men listened to
her gay conversation with smiling encouragement; they found it an enjoyable relaxation.
Her style of narration was very dramatic and
vivid, and they did not stop to inquire whether
there was any solid basis, or, in fact, any foun-
dation at all, for her prettily told stories; and
if any Miss Brown gave a doubtful shrug, or
uttered a word of disbelief, she found an apol-
ogist before her. She was the life of the
company she happened to be in, and everybody
voted her charming — a little given to embel-
lishment, perhaps; but that was owing to her
enthusiastic nature. She was an incessant
talker, and had read a good deal — very super-
ficially, it is true; but as long as she was
bright and amusing, people were satisfied.
She took a wonderful interest in the individ-
ual she happened to be talking with at the

moment, and she succeeded in making that person believe that he or she was the one being in the world in whose society she took the greatest delight — excepting, perhaps, Miss Brown, who could not believe that one pair of arms could take in the whole world. But Miss Brown was only Miss Brown, and nobody paid any attention to her. But it was well for the Widow Wyse that she had a mother who knew her weakness in the way of making promises only to break them.

"When are you going to arrange for the bazar in aid of the 'Poor Fund,' Julia?" asked Mrs. Houlton, as her daughter made a late appearance at the breakfast-table one morning. "It will not do to disappoint the rector."

"Good gracious, mamma! I had forgotten his very existence," said Mrs. Wyse. "I believe I did promise to do something, and of course I must. I wish the rector, the church, and the poor, were in Guinea."

"You shouldn't be so reckless in your promises," said her mother, laughing at her ludicrous look of disgust. "I do really wish you would be more careful, Julia. I never was more embarrassed in my life than I was last week when young Eaton came, by your invitation, to dinner. You told me nothing about it, and, when he spoke of you, I said you were out, I did not know where. Of course I made the best of it when he told me you expected him to dine with you, and said that you would doubtless explain your absence."

"Which I did, to his entire satisfaction, the next day. I said I was called away hastily to see a person who was ill, and for the time forgot even him. The last part of my statement was perfectly true," said Mrs. Wyse, laughing. "Of course he forgave me, and gave me credit for my quick sympathies, besides."

Her mother smiled, and said, finally : —

"I really think, my dear, that it would do you no harm to take an interest in the church, now. You have been very gay, and people will think you frivolous if you go on, which would never do, you know."

"You are right, as usual, mamma," answered her daughter. "Fortunately it is almost Lent, so I should have to be sedate soon, anyway.

We can do a good deal in six weeks, and we will have a grand fair at Easter. I shall manage the whole thing, and do myself credit. Mr. Aden will be delighted. Just fancy what a saint he will think me," and she laughed softly at the thought. "I shall not tire myself with work, I assure you. You must help me; and I will interest the old tabbies, so that they will do something besides talk; and the girls will do anything I ask of them."

It was a new excitement, and she rushed into it with her whole heart.

"I shall ask Charlotte Brown to luncheon to-morrow, to talk the matter over and see what she will do; and I want you to be more than civil to her," she went on, with enthusiasm.

"But why do you ask Charlotte Brown? There are a good many girls more agreeable than she," said Mrs. Houlton.

"Oh, mamma!" exclaimed the politic Julia, "I do really sometimes think you a trifle dull. Don't you know that Miss Brown is one of the *substantials* of this little town — one who is to be thoroughly depended upon, who dotes on the rector and Mrs. Aden — a pillar of the church, so to speak? She has been rather snubbed by the young ladies lately, I should say, and she must be coaxed. I shall make her adore me before the affair is over."

And Mrs. Wyse ordered her carriage. She met Miss Brown coming out of her own door.

"Oh, Lottie!" she said, "I am so glad that I did n't quite miss you. No, dear, I cannot come in this morning; but I want to see you particularly, on church matters. We must not always be gay, you know, and I think it is high time that I, at least, should be doing something useful; but I am inexperienced, and I want your help and advice. I dare say, you are going on some errand of mercy now. You are so good always, even when you are the gayest, that you make me ashamed." And she wiped away an imaginary tear. "Lottie, dear, cannot you come and discuss the matter with me over a cup of coffee to-morrow, at one? Indeed, you must, for I cannot do anything without you. Of course the young girls will do a good deal after everything is planned; but young ladies who are not giddy must direct them. We have helped them to enjoy a good deal during the winter, and now we must make them work."

Ah, Widow Wyse! you are indeed a clever schemer. You have taken at least ten years from Miss Brown. It is very evident that *you* do not think her old. It is something, too, to hear the popular Widow Wyse say, " *We* will do so and so." She has not been called by her pet name for years. Even her mother calls her Charlotte now, and she is Miss Brown to everybody else. You know very well that "Lottie, dear," will do for you what plain Miss Brown would not.

Of course the fair was a success. The Widow Wyse and Miss Brown presided over the flower temple, and nobody passed by without a call and a purchase. They succeeded in astonishing everybody with the amount of money they took. The fair widow would not do anything without her dear Lottie. She was so attentive to her that she compelled attention from others; for all of which Miss Brown was grateful. The skilful Ninette had

dressed her hair for the occasion, and she did
indeed look and feel younger and fairer than
she had done for years. Her cheeks flushed
with pleasure as Mrs. Wyse whispered, with
an admiring look : —

"You are lovely to-night, dear. Always do
your hair just as it is now. It is very
becoming."

And she declared to her mother, when she
returned home that night, that she had mis-
judged Mrs. Wyse ; she had thought her vain
and frivolous, but she was an earnest, whole-
souled woman.

And this "earnest, whole-souled woman"
got all the credit. She had given some handsome embroideries and a few Swiss carvings
for the fancy-table, and had encouraged Charlotte Brown to work and organize and engineer
the whole thing, while she fluttered from one
to another, and praised, flattered, or cajoled,
as seemed necessary.

Her mother said, the next morning : —

"That was a very clever idea of yours, my
dear, of interesting Miss Brown. She worked
hard, and was a most excellent foil for you."

Mrs. Wyse only smiled.

The rector was profoundly grateful. Indeed he told her that he could hardly express his thanks that she, who was almost a stranger, should take such an interest in the parish.

"Oh, dear Mr. Aden! don't call me a stranger," she said, the ready tears springing to her eyes. "I have been feeling that I was at home. I have been so busy and so happy that I had almost forgotten the few years"—

The dismayed rector impulsively seized her hand, and said, rather incoherently:—

"I am so glad—I mean—that you are here. You have been so kind and thoughtful, and—and—I shall bring Mrs. Aden to see you very soon."

While the widow thought: "How charming this would be, were there no Mrs. Aden! It is a great mistake for a young, interesting clergyman to marry."

Mrs. Wyse, by her manner, always gave people to understand that there had been something wanting in her married life. That it had not been one of perfect happiness. The young girls, overhearing snatches of

conversations concerning it, said : " They say
he was perfectly horrid," meaning the late
Archibald Wyse, but nobody in Alliance knew
anything about the matter, excepting what
they could gather from Mrs. Houlton's vague
hints, which were always, of course, to her
daughter's credit.

CHAPTER X.

CHRISTMAS coming on Tuesday, the young ladies of Madam Leonard's were permitted to go home on the previous Saturday. Ethel spent Sunday with Kitty, and on Monday, much to that young lady's chagrin went to pay the promised visit to Mr. Apthorpe. She received a most cordial welcome. The house had a holiday appearance, and there was an eager, expectant look upon the faces of its inmates. It was seen even in the eyes of the tawny, splendid-looking St. Bernard, which walked majestically into the room to greet her. He was followed by two lesser specimens of the canine species. It was amusing to see the tiny white Maltese terrier look reverently up to his big companion.

"Is he not a noble fellow?" said Mr. Apthorpe, calling her attention to the first-mentioned dog. "Do you notice the almost human look in his eyes? He is disappointed, poor fellow. I believe he thought it was Jed. No, old fellow, you'll hardly see him until evening. I need not ask if you are fond of dogs, Miss Ethel. I can see it in your eyes."

"I love them," said Ethel, enthusiastically, "and I miss my own sadly. I shall make friends with His Majesty at once," stroking the head of the fine fellow beside her. "How handsome he is!"

"Yes," answered Mr. Apthorpe, "and so intelligent. Why, he almost talks. We are all very fond of him, and care for him as if he were a child. He has a regular bed, and lays his head upon a pillow every night. I am glad you like dogs. It will be a strong bond of sympathy between us. But I see Eleanor is waiting to take you to your room. I hope you will be comfortable and happy, my dear."

"I am sure I shall be," said Ethel, gratefully, as she followed Mrs. Amesbury to her room.

"Now, my dear," said her hostess, who always made it a point to see, personally, that her guests were comfortable, "pray, make yourself thoroughly at home. My brother insists upon the largest liberty, not only for himself, but also for his friends. If you should wish to be alone, you can be without apology, but the whole house is open to you, with one exception. Whenever you find the door of my brother's 'den' closed, you may know that he wishes to be alone. If it is open, go in freely, for it is a sign of invitation. Now, I will leave you, and send my own maid to assist you."

She started downstairs, but came back to say: "I forgot to tell you that I have to go out this morning; you will not mind it, I am sure. You will find my brother below, and luncheon is served at two. I may not be back for it, but it is a wholly informal meal."

Ethel had little need of a maid, and soon dismissed her, and after making herself present-able, went down to find her host, who, hearing her step, called out: "Come into my den! my dear. I want you to see where I spend most of my time."

Ethel entered, and found Mr. Apthorpe seated in a large library surrounded by his dogs, books, and papers, and as she glanced hastily around upon the large cases of handsomely bound books, the lovely oil paintings, fine statuary, and in-viting easy-chairs, she said, laughingly: —

"A rather luxurious den, I should say. You evidently have no sympathy with asceticism."

"No," he answered, "I confess to a liking for the good things of this life. I believe they were given us to enjoy. I do not believe in voluntary penance. There are plenty of hard things that we are forced to suffer. Sin inevitably brings its punishment, and there is no one upon earth that is free from it. But I won't preach you a sermon, for it is hardly my forte, but instead I will show you some fine paintings that I picked up in my wanderings."

Everything about this elegant house stamped its owner as a man of the most delicate and refined taste. Ethel felt that she was in an enchanted castle, whose good genius had cast a spell over her. Mr. Apthorpe was in his happiest mood, and Ethel listened with a strange, intense delight to his wholly charming conversation. She had associated with men of culture all her life. Her father was a superior man in all respects, and she was his especial pride and constant companion. Few girls had her privileges of association. She was a girl of rare good sense, and while enjoying dancing and other gay amusements thoroughly, she was not frivolous, and she recognized at once her host's superiority. He had, indeed, been endowed with great mental gifts. He was a deep student of science and literature, and a writer of great force and strength, and a man so intellectual, so versatile, with such ready wit, could hardly fail of compelling from a girl of Ethel's temperament a sort of worshipful admiration. She pleased him, too, by her quick sympathy. Her manner of listening was full of graceful intelligence, which drew from him his best thoughts. Indeed, it was a day of perfect enjoyment for Ethel. And it was refreshing to Richard Apthorpe to find his friend's beautiful daughter so fresh and unspoiled.

There were many points of resemblance between Mr. Apthorpe and Dr. Townsend, though the former was intellectually stronger and far more gifted. Ethel had had implanted in her inmost soul an intense hatred of shams and an utter contempt for anything that seemed like deception. The white light of a beautiful soul shone in her eyes, and no one looking into their clear depths could have a suspicion that the smallest amount of deceit could find a lodging-place in her heart.

She was astonished when Mr. Apthorpe led the way to the dining-room where luncheon was spread.

" It cannot be two o'clock," she said, glancing toward the mantel.

" Just ten minutes past," said Mr. Apthorpe, smiling at her look of surprise.

After luncheon, which he took standing, Mr. Apthorpe said : —

" Now, my dear, if you are not tired of the sound of my voice, I will read some of my own poems to you ; but first, I must show you a little painting that suggested the idea of one of them to me."

It was a delicious bit of the gorgeous East. A dark-eyed houri had thrown herself with delightful abandon upon a luxurious couch. A perfect picture of careless, unstudied grace. Ethel stood before it as if fascinated.

"Do you like it ?" he asked, at length, finding that she did not speak.

" It is perfect," she answered. " Do tell me, who was the artist ? He was inspired when he painted that picture."

"It is one of my own," he answered, carelessly. "I am glad you like it, for it is one of
my favorites."

She stopped short, as they were about enter-
ing the library door, and asked, incredulously:
"Do you mean that you painted it yourself?"

"Yes. Why not?" he answered, smiling at
her peculiar manner.

"Mr. Apthorpe," she said, with ridiculous
solemnity, "I am positively afraid of you.
Can you really do everything?"

"Indeed, I cannot!" he answered quickly,
"or I should change some people I know."
Then he added, more seriously: "I ought to
show something of which may be said, 'Well
done!' for I have had great opportunities."

He went to one of the bookcases and took
down a small volume, saying, —

"Now, my dear, make yourself comfortable,
upon that lounge, while I soothe you with a
song."

As she lay there listening in dreamy content-
ment to the smoothly flowing lines, her small
hands clasped above her head, with its golden
crown, drawing back the close sleeve and

revealing the beautifully rounded arms, Richard Apthorpe thought he had never seen a fairer picture.

"If I could only paint her as she is now," he thought, "what a companion I could make for the Eastern scene she admires so much!"

In the meantime Mrs. Amesbury had returned and had glanced into the library several times unobserved.

She was a lady of great tact and kindness of heart, and when her guests were happy, she very wisely let them alone. Ethel felt thoroughly at home from the first. She saw that that was what they desired, and that there was to be no labored attempt to entertain her. Everything was naturally, easily, and gracefully done.

"Do you think we may expect Gerald in season for dinner?" asked Mrs. Amesbury, a little anxiously, as she looked in a little later.

"He may come on the six-ten," answered her brother, "though probably not until a later train. It is strange he did not telegraph, but," a little impatiently, "Jed is such a careless fellow."

"I don't think Gerald is careless," answered his sister. "He has probably sent a telegram You know, there is sometimes a delay in the delivery. We will delay dinner a little."

But dinner-time came and went, and Gerald did not make his appearance. Indeed he had not done so when Ethel retired for the night, which she did early, saying that she was tired, that the brother and sister might be alone to greet the returned traveler.

"What a lovely girl she is," remarked Mrs. Amesbury, as she left the room.

"She is, indeed," answered her brother. "I find her very intelligent and appreciative, with an opinion clearly her own. I notice the same disposition to analyze people that is one of her father's characteristics. Her criticisms are very keen, too. I should recognize her as Ned Townsend's daughter, anywhere. We used to say in college that his scalpel was always at hand."

"He is a physician, is he not?" asked Mrs. Amesbury.

"Yes," answered Mr. Apthorpe, "but being wealthy by inheritance, he has never practised,

except to give his services to those who were
too poor to pay for them. He is a noble-
hearted man, and I have always been very fond
of him, although I have not seen him for a
number of years. We must try and make little
Ethel happy. I am glad Jed is to be here."

"Yes," answered his sister. "Gerald can
do so much to make her visit pleasant."

Ethel was greeted the next morning, as she
drew back the curtains, with a burst of sunshine. It was a bright, glorious morning, but
she did not leave her chamber until the last
moment; indeed it was not until the house-
maid had announced breakfast at her door,
that she slowly descended. She met Mr.
Apthorpe as he was passing through the hall
to the drawing-room, but his answer to her
pleasant greeting was quite unintelligible. A
little surprised at his coldness, she followed
him, remarking upon the beautiful morning.

"Is it?" he growled. "I had not noticed it."

She looked at him in wonder, saying,
anxiously, "Are you ill, dear Mr. Apthorpe?"

"Oh, no," he answered, a little more gently,
"I am not ill, my dear, but I am not as young

as I once was, and when I feel twinges of rheumatism I am made painfully aware of it."

She passed into the breakfast-room, and finding Mrs. Amesbury alone, said : —

"I fear that Mr. Apthorpe is feeling very ill. He does n't seem at all like himself, this morning."

"Oh, he is not ill," said Mrs. Amesbury, smiling : "he is only disappointed, that is all. You are to take no notice of it, my dear. You know, we expected Gerald last night, but instead of our brother, came a letter, which had in some unaccountable way been delayed, saying that it was very uncertain when he would be home, as he was about to join a party of English friends who were going to Egypt. We are very fond of Gerald, and it is a great disappointment."

"Mr. Gerald is a great traveler, is he not?" asked Ethel, feeling that she must say something.

"Oh, yes, both of my brothers are fond of travel, and Gerald has been abroad a good part of the time in the last five or six years. I wanted you to know him. He is very clever, and such a charming talker."

"Is he like Mr. Apthorpe?" asked Ethel, feeling sure that he could not be.

"Oh, no, indeed! They are totally unlike. You would **never** dream that they belonged to the same family," said Mrs. Amesbury.

"Does n't Major Apthorpe like Boston?" asked Ethel, trying to seem interested.

"Oh! for that matter," said Mrs. Amesbury, "to hear him discourse upon that subject you would think that he considered it one of the most delightful places on the face of the earth. Oh, yes! Gerald has a proper reverence for Boston, only it happens that we are not able to keep him here long at a time."

At that moment Mr. Apthorpe, who appeared to be in no hurry for his breakfast, came in. He was in what his sister called one of his "moods." Nothing seemed to exactly please him. He found fault with the air, which was too sharp, when he was out for his regular morning walk. The sun was too bright: it dazzled his eyes; and the breakfast was hardly to his taste. Finally, in looking over the morning paper, he found something which worked him up to what he called a state of "righteous indignation," when he felt better.

A few people had been invited to dinner, and Ethel found that she had been bidden to a rich intellectual feast, for at Richard Apthorpe's dinner-table the talk was always of the best and the wit the keenest. His arrangement of the means of hospitality was perfect. His dinners were good, and he had that rare social instinct which enabled him always to select those who were congenial to each other. Occasionally, to be sure, as in the present case, a disturbing element would creep in ; but it was always an accident.

Professor Aiken, an old acquaintance, had dropped in, and was invited to stay. He was a man so impressed with the idea of his own importance that he could see nothing beyond it. He had been asked, not without design, to take Ethel in to dinner. Mr. Apthorpe said to his sister, while passing : —

"I want to see him try to overawe little Ethel. She will show him his mistake, I fancy."

Ethel was at first amused at his condescend-

ing manner, and his evident efforts to come
down to her small comprehension, as he questioned her about her school and studies; but
she soon tired of his trivial remarks, and
showed her annoyance plainly, for she was
losing a good deal of the brilliancy around her.
He persisted, however, in talking, taking himself for a subject, on which he seemed perfectly
at home. He took up the whole time in
explaining to her by what means he had
arrived at his present exalted position.

Mr. Apthorpe smiled, as they finally left the
table, to see a bright spot, indicative of sup-
pressed wrath, on Ethel's cheeks. It seemed
that the professor felt that he had not sufficiently impressed her with his importance,
for she could not get rid of him. He kept
persistently by her side after their return to
the drawing-room. Finally Mr. Apthorpe
heard, with satisfaction, two or three sharp
retorts from the long-suffering Ethel, which
seemed not only to surprise, but to offend, the
wise professor, and there was a flash of sympathy in his eyes which was not lost upon his
young guest.

"Well, my dear," said Mr. Apthorpe, teasingly, the next morning, "I noticed that you were enjoying a discussion with Professor Aiken last evening. What do you think of him?"

"I hardly like to say," answered Ethel. "You know I never saw him before."

"Ah! but you are quick to form an opinion; let us have it," said he.

"Well, if you really wish to know," she answered, flushing, partly with amusement and partly with anger, at the remembrance of said "discussion," "he seems to look at everybody through the large end of the glass. They seem to him very small, as well as a long way from him. The letter *I* is, with him, the most important one in the whole alphabet. He is a tenacious old bulldog, holding on to his opinions, right or wrong, with a grip which says, 'I will die before I will let go.' And being a dear little white cat, I was, of course, true to my nature; I arched my back, spit at him, scratched him, and worried him generally, until he was glad to leave me, dragging his old opinions after him. He evidently thought my own of very little consequence, and I should not have quarreled with him for that, had he let me alone; but I am not in the habit of being patronized. But, really," she went on, after a little pause, "you must have been ashamed of me; I was ashamed of myself. I did n't know I could be so belligerent. There was so little to arouse my blood in the languid South that I fancied myself amiable. I am afraid I do not appreciate your friend as he thinks he deserves. Perhaps I was on the wrong side of him. I might have been awed, had I not espied, beneath his dignified garb, the stilts peeping out. I am willing and glad to look up to a man who towers, standing grandly on his feet; but if he be mounted on stilts, let him look out," with a sudden motion of the hand, as though she would sweep away the imaginary stilts.

Mr. Apthorpe laughed, saying, —

"You are your papa's own daughter, my dear."

"I am glad to have you say that," answered Ethel, "for I am very proud of papa."

"You have good reason to be," said Mr.

Apthorpe; "and I, too, am proud of his friendship. He is worthy of any man's admiration."

"But why is it," she went on, "that that man should arouse all the antagonism in my nature?"

"I cannot say," he answered; "but I understand your feelings perfectly. He often attacks me in the same way."

"*You?*" said Ethel, with an incredulous look. "How does he dare to do that? You are as much above him as heaven is above the earth."

He could not mistake the genuineness of her admiration, and, appreciated and admired as he had always justly been by all whose opinions were worth having, his heart was touched as it had never been before, and he kissed her, softly saying, —

"I wish we could keep you with us always, my dear;" and she answered: —

"It seems strange that you should care for a simple girl like me, but I believe you do, and it makes me very happy."

There was a tear in Richard Apthorpe's eye,

as she left the room, but he dashed it
impatiently away with the irrelevant exclamation : —

"Why the devil Jed can't come home and
live like a Christian, instead of roving about
the world like a veritable Bohemian, I cannot
understand!"

He was a strange mixture of tenderness and
inflexibility, of sweetness and acidity. Terribly
fascinating in his anger, and very lovable in his
moments of tender thoughtfulness for the
happiness of others.

Ethel did not try to analyze her feelings.
She was happy, in a dreamy contented sort of
way, with an undefined hope that this pleasant
life might last forever. She was thoroughly
at her ease, and she was thankful, selfishly
thankful, that the supercilious Gerald's return
had been indefinitely postponed. She felt
sorry for the disappointment of his family, for
they were absurdly fond of him, but as Lizzie
Highgate would say : —

"It was just too awfully convenient for her."

CHAPTER XI.

HOLIDAY PLEASURES.

"My Poor, Neglected Papa, — My conscience upbraids me for having allowed my pen to lie idle so long, but do not imagine for a moment that you have been out of my mind. I think of you always and long for some good genius to transport you hither in the twinkling of an eye, as in the days of Aladdin the wonderful. I wish you could know how much I am enjoying in this lovely home. I came on Monday, and every moment has been one of happiness. Mrs. Amesbury received me with open arms, and Mr. Apthorpe has been delightful. You said he had a heart of gold, and you said truly. His mind is stored with diamonds and pearls and all sorts of lovely and precious things, which are continually dropping from his lips. Congratulate me, dear papa, on my good-fortune in being here to catch them as they fall. But he does not believe in casting pearls before swine. He does not show his jewels to everybody. It is only when he is surrounded by those he likes that he shows how thoroughly charming he can be. I do not flatter myself that it is because of anything he sees in me to admire, that he is so kind, but because of his friendship for you. Thank you, dear, for condescending to be my father. Mr. Apthorpe is the most unconsciously bright man I ever met. But sometimes he is very severe. Mrs. Amesbury calls him her two-edged sword. Nana Cleveland says that he is a perfect lion when aroused, and that he can not only growl, but he can roar so terrifically that he can be heard all over the country. But he has not frightened me yet. He has been most kind and considerate in every way. What a wonderfully fascinating man he is! He says that he has had great opportunities, and I am sure he has never let any of them escape him. It is the intensity of his utterances that makes him seem so aggressive. He is always ready when occasion calls for rebuke, and then his accents fall upon the ear so clear and keen and stinging they seem electrical. One could imagine him in the thickest of the affray of battle, and with all-controlling power hurling with tones of thunder the squadrons on to victory, combating successfully what would seem to others a forlorn hope. He would be a prominent man anywhere. His towering intellect makes him seem a giant among men. There is something grand in his denunciations of wrong-doing, but I should not want to be the culprit standing before him.

"I should not speak so freely to any one else, but I am sure that you, who know him so well, will not think me too enthusiastic. The remembrance of this visit will last until I make another, for I am to come again, and render me superior to the small annoyances of school life. I shall write again, very soon, dear papa, but just now I am too full of one subject to write on any other.

"Your loving

"TEDDY."

At this moment there was a slight knock at the door, followed by some one rushing in and seizing Ethel in her arms. It was Kitty, whom she had not seen since the Monday before.

"I have come to carry you off!" she said; "mamma is to give a stupid little reception for some school boys and teachers this evening, and she insisted on my helping her to entertain them, so I insist upon your coming to help me. You won't have to dress; come, put on your hat and wrap. I have explained it all to your friends below and they say that I may have you if I will bring you back to-morrow, which I shall do unless," she said mischievously, "you should wish to stay and have a cup of tea with the malcontents."

"And who are the 'malcontents'?" asked Ethel.

"Why, don't you know?" asked Kitty. "They are those women who are not satisfied with that state of life in which it has pleased God to place them. They meet every month to talk over their grievances, and state their 'views' to their sisters in affliction, and try to devise some means to soften their hard-hearted masters, or what they would like better, to compel them to give up the reins of government to them. They are like little children, who, thinking their little hands sufficiently strong, are crying to drive the horses. As if women couldn't do mischief enough without the ballot!"

"Does your mamma believe in woman's suffrage?" asked Ethel.

"To a certain extent," answered Kitty, "and they hope to win her over completely."

"But those poor boys weigh heavily on my mind. I suppose they are thinking about their neckties now, and they will work themselves into a state of positive agony before evening. I told mamma that it was an act of cruelty on her part to invite them, but she thinks they will enjoy it. I didn't take the carriage, for I thought you might like to walk."

"I should like it very much," answered Ethel, "as I have not been out of the house to-day."

They had a long, delightful walk and reached the house just as it was being lighted for the evening.

Mrs. Brewster met Ethel with a kiss of welcome, saying, —

"It is very good of you to come, my dear. You must both of you try to make the young

men feel at their ease. I know that you do
not need to be cautioned," she went on, turning to Ethel, "but I am always a little apprehensive with regard to my mischievous Kitten."

" I 'll be as serious as a judge presiding over
a murder trial," said the irrepressible Kitty.

" No, my dear," said Mrs. Brewster, smiling ;
"I wish you to be neither very serious nor
yet giddy, but perfectly natural."

" Just hear her ! " said Kitty, mischief dancing in her brown eyes. " She wants me to be
'perfectly natural!' Yet my natural state is
such that she is 'constantly apprehensive.' I
call that unconscionably unreasonable. Mamma
does n't know that the last time she had such
a gathering I was deliberately awkward, just
to put one poor fellow at his ease, and I am
sure kindness to animals could go no farther
than that, and yet that very evening she
threatened me with the nursery just because
she fancied I was amused at something."

" I don't know what I should do without
that nursery," said Mrs. Brewster, laughing.
" I do really have to send Kitty there now,
occasionally."

Mrs. Brewster was a gracious hostess and the young men felt at ease with her always, but mischievous Kitty unconsciously played sad havoc with their too susceptible hearts. They belonged to a university in which Mrs. Brewster was very much interested, and they received many proofs of that lady's kind thoughtfulness from time to time.

Kitty managed to meet Ethel alone during the evening and said hurriedly : —

" Well, dear, what do you think of mamma's pets ? They remind me of those mechanical dolls which can bend, and manage to articulate something like words, if they are squeezed. If a pretty girl speaks to one of them, it puts him in torture, which answers to the squeezing, and he mumbles an unintelligible word or two. How I pity the poor things ! and mamma really thinks they enjoy it."

" I imagined myself in a bowling-alley," said Ethel. "They were all standing in such straight, solemn rows, that I could n't help wishing for a bowl. I am sure if I could have had one, they would all have gone down together."

"Oh! that is very good," said Kitty. "I must tell mamma of that."

"Not for the world," said Ethel. "She would not threaten me with the nursery, but she would send me there at once, and serve me right, too. Go to your duty, my dear. I am going to talk to that poor boy, who is twisting his fingers off in the corner."

There were the usual number of accidents at the supper-table. Ethel was amused to see, as one young gentleman let a dish of ice-cream slip out of his hand, that Kitty quick as thought dropped hers, and said to her companion, loud enough for the unlucky fellow to hear : —

"Don't let mamma know, for I do really want her to think that I have got through one evening without dropping anything."

And the next morning, as she saw her mamma looking ruefully at a large spot on her handsome carpet, she said, with mock seriousness : —

"I did it, mamma, with my little dish of cream, for I knew that you would rather have forty grease spots than that one poor boy should feel awkward."

Mr. Brewster, who was standing near, laughed heartily, saying, —

"That's right, Kittikin. It is the kind of charity which covers a multitude of sins; you are growing more like your mamma every day."

Ethel returned to the Apthorpes' the next morning in a drizzle of rain and sleet, her hands full of lovely roses.

"My dear," said Mr. Apthorpe, "I thought it was stormy; but you have brought us sunshine."

"I have brought some roses to light up your den," said Ethel. "Are they not lovely?"

"Indeed they are," he answered, "and I will enjoy them by-and-by. I have to go down town for an hour or two. In the meantime, if you are in the mood for reading, here is a French novel that I have been looking over; you will find it bright and amusing. I believe Eleanor is busy."

Ethel took the book to her room, and was soon oblivious to everything else. The next day, which was stormy also, she spent quietly

within doors; but on Monday came sunshine —
a clear, cold day. She took a brisk walk in the
morning, and after luncheon she went out with
Mrs. Amesbury for a little shopping.

"I am going to the florist's first," said Mrs.
Amesbury. "We are to have a few friends
this evening — only a small company, my dear:
the Brewsters and a few others; and I want
you to select the flowers."

"Oh, that will be delightful!" said Ethel.
"I am sure Kitty will enjoy it as much as I
shall."

That evening, about ten o'clock, as Ethel
had strayed away from the others, and was
standing before an odd carving, whose hideous
grotesqueness had often fascinated her, she
heard Mrs. Amesbury's voice saying, —

"Ah! here she is."

She looked up quickly, as her hostess said:
"Ethel, my dear, this is my brother Gerald.
Miss Townsend — Gerald," and saw, as she
acknowledged the introduction, a young man
of medium height, with smiling blue eyes and
blonde whiskers, cut in the English style,
who, bowing with much grace, expressed his
pleasure at meeting her,

"I hope we shall be friends, Miss Town-send," he said. "My brother has spoken of you in his letters, and I have heard so much of your father from him that I felt that I scarcely needed an introduction."

Fortunately for Ethel, at that moment he excused himself at a call from his brother. She was, for once in her life, greatly embarrassed.

"So this is the elegant Major Apthorpe," she soliloquized, as he turned away. "I wonder when he came. I am sure they did not expect him; or, if they did, they wanted to surprise me. Not a very pleasant surprise, I am sure. What an 'idjet' he must have thought me, as I stood staring at him."

"Well, my dear," said Mrs. Amesbury, coming back to her, "you see Gerald has returned, and it was such a surprise. He walked in about ten minutes ago, as though it were the most natural thing in the world."

"But he is in evening-dress," said Ethel, surprised out of her usual politeness.

"Ah, yes!" answered Mrs. Amesbury; "that is like Gerald. He is always prepared

for an emergency. He carries a dress-suit
with him always; and as he came up to the
house he noticed that there was company, so
he drove to the hotel, made himself present-
able, and came back. I was so astonished!
You see, this party of friends gave up their
intended visit to Egypt because two of their
number were obliged to return to England on
account of the death of a relative; so we have
Gerald, after all, and it will be a very ' Happy
New Year' for us; but let us go back to the
drawing-room."

Ethel's eyes were irresistibly drawn toward
Major Apthorpe, who was, of course, the
centre of attraction. She noticed this carefully costumed young man from the points of
his spotless collar to the tips of his dainty,
perfectly fitting boots, and she said to herself : —

"Kitty is right. He certainly is ' nice.' "

As she drew nearer she noticed that he had
a low, musical voice, and that he compelled
attention by his earnest way of presenting a
subject. His perfect courtesy and high breed-
ing were noticeable, even among the cultivated

people present. She was beginning to soften toward him, and to feel as though she had done him an injustice, when a voice at her side aroused her, and brought back all her unreasonable prejudice.

"Do you see how Major Apthorpe is enjoying the sensation he has made, Miss Townsend?"

It was Nana Cleveland who spoke.

"It is quite like a play, is it not?" Ethel answered, a little coldly. "Major Apthorpe's return was very unexpected to his friends."

"My dear Miss Townsend," said Miss Cleveland, "Major Apthorpe is in the habit of doing unexpected things. It adds to the general interest concerning him. You will notice that when people are speaking of him every sentence ends with an exclamation point when it does n't with an interrogation."

Ethel laughed.

"Is he really such an egotist as you represent him?" she asked.

"Oh! you must judge for yourself. You are likely to have an opportunity," said Miss Cleveland, as she moved away.

"At all events," thought Ethel, "he shall have nothing from me upon which to feed his vanity."

A few minutes later, as she stood listening to the hum of well-bred voices, where Nana had left her, she heard that young lady's voice a little above the rest, and slightly acrimonious, talking to Major Apthorpe. She noticed a slight vein of sarcasm running through his conversation with her, and she also noticed "that air of fine disdain" which Nana had spoken of.

"How bitter she is toward him," said Ethel to herself. "One could almost imagine her to be in love with him, she seems to hate him so."

CHAPTER XII.

ETHEL was awakened the next morning by the joyful barking of the dogs. She heard a door open, and a soft, caressing voice as the petted animals tumbled pellmell into the room.

"Everybody seems to love him," she thought, "except Nana, and I am not perfectly sure that she does not."

They met at breakfast, but Major Apthorpe addressed little of his conversation to her. He talked with his brother concerning his travels and their mutual friends abroad. After breakfast both brothers went out, and Ethel settled herself in the library with a magazine, hoping to have a quiet time by herself. A few minutes later, however, Major Apthorpe walked in, saying, as he rubbed his cold hands : —

"These chilly mornings must make you long for your Southern home, Miss Townsend."

He possessed an exquisite charm, — a grace

of manner as rare as it was pleasing, and it was impossible that Ethel should not feel its influence.

"Oh, no," she answered, "I like the North. I have Northern blood in my veins, which I feel in this crisp, exhilarating air to the very tips of my fingers; but, oh! I do miss my roses, my big, luscious roses." She checked herself quickly, for she did not mean to show any part of herself to this man of the world, this cold-hearted, polished cynic. He should not look upon her as a gushing school-girl. He noticed her sudden change of manner, and smiled, saying to himself :—

"Very pretty, but decidedly capricious."

There was a conflict in her mind an hour later, as, hearing a step, she looked up just as a shower of roses came down upon her book, and she looked into Gerald Apthorpe's laughing eyes, as he said :—

"Imagine yourself in the Sunny South, Miss Townsend. Here are sunshine, warmth, flowers. What more can you ask for?"

Her first feeling was of anger against herself, him, and the poor flowers; but it passed away, and she took them up saying, gently, —

"They are very beautiful. Thank you, but I did not mean to ask for them."

"And you did not," he answered. "I love flowers, too, and I mean to enjoy these with you. Shall I put them in water?"

He called a servant, who brought a vase filled with water. He noticed that she retained a few, which she placed in her corsage, and said to himself : —

"If she does n't throw them away in a pet at the end of five minutes, I suppose I ought to be profoundly grateful. I wonder that Dick should have taken such an amazing fancy to her. He must have looked at her through his artistic eye. She is uncommonly pretty."

Although for the next few days Ethel could not help acknowledging to herself that this self-sufficient young man was very thoughtful for her comfort in a quiet, unobtrusive sort of way, she meant to be constantly on her guard lest she should seem to have fallen under that charm of manner of which he himself was evidently as fully conscious as his admiring friends. Cool indifference was what she aimed at, but she often forgot herself, thus strengthening his first estimate of her that she was a spoiled beauty, capricious, vain, and coquettish. He did not trouble her with his society. Indeed, at first she saw but little of him. He was full of plans and projects which he talked over with his brother, and seemed sometimes almost unaware of her presence. He was at times provokingly indifferent. His mind seemed completely engrossed with business affairs.

Major Apthorpe had never been so foolish as to fall in love in the whole course of his life. He enjoyed his popularity, and why should he not? There was a certain magnetism about him that was irresistible to men as well as to women. The efforts of managing mammas to secure so eligible a *parti* for their daughters were evident to everybody, and extremely amusing to observers; for he was perfectly heart-whole, strongly fortified at all points, and he took no pains to conceal the fact. The truth is, he was too fastidious to feel quite satisfied with the modern society belle, but there was, deep down in his heart, a sweet, womanly ideal, with which he compared each young lady who had at all interested him, and the verdict so far had been : "Tried and found wanting."

The mammas said : "He is not a marrying man"; each one at the same time secretly hoping to find some weak point to assail. No one could call him a fop, but his taste in matters of dress was simply perfect. He was "nice," from the crown of his well-balanced head to the tips of his daintily shod feet. He had, as I have said, polished, delightful manners, a sweet, persuasive voice, and seemed able to sway his hearers whithersoever he would. He was not a man of wild and reckless theories, though an untiring enthusiast, who put his whole soul into his work, and though slender of frame, his physical endurance was remarkable. It was the buoyancy of his spirits which made him, no matter what fatigue he had undergone, always fresh, gay, debonair, entertaining his friends always with the same airy ease and elegance. But he could be gay without being dissolute. Gerald Apthorpe's character was above reproach.

Ethel was wont to ensconce herself in a corner of the sofa in the library, with her

book, when Mr. Apthorpe was absent, and
one morning, the latter part of the week, she
had been reading an hour or more when
Major Apthorpe, whom she had imagined out
as usual at that time of the day, walked
leisurely in, with a lighted cigar between his
lips, which he threw away on discovering her
presence.

"I have disturbed you," he said; "shall I
go away?"

"Oh, no," she answered. "I am glad to
shut my book. I have read too long already.
But why do you waste good cigars in this
prodigal fashion? That is the second one
you have thrown away this morning."

"I thought it might be disagreeable to you;
besides, I would rather talk with you than
smoke," he said, gallantly. "I am not wedded
to cigars."

"You can smoke and talk, too," she answered.
"It would not trouble me in the least; indeed,
I rather like the flavor of a cigar. Papa is
always smoking, and we are constantly together when at home. And do you know,"
she added, mischievously, "that Southern ladies
sometimes smoke?"

"Ah," he said, with the slightest possible curl of the lip, "perhaps I have been remiss. May I offer you a cigarette? Will you smoke with me?"

"Not for the world," answered Ethel, quickly. "I think the habit unladylike in the extreme."

"Then I shall not smoke," he said, decidedly. "What are you reading? Ah, I see. You must be devoted to history, to read it during the holidays."

"I detest it heartily," she answered. "It is a self-imposed daily task, though I really got interested this morning, for a wonder. But I am hopeless, as far as names and dates are concerned. Madam Leonard considers me a positive disgrace in this respect. There are only two dates that I make any pretence of remembering. They are 1492 and 1812. I know there was a war in one, and a discovery in the other; but I sometimes get them mixed. I do, indeed. I wonder if there is any way to cultivate the memory. What 's-his-name has said — I dare say you remember who, I am sure I do not — that the mind is like a sieve: the more it is crowded, the larger the holes become. You can imagine how mine has been crammed, since everything runs through."

Major Apthorpe laughed, and said : " Tell me about your school. Who is Madam Leonard, and do you like her ? "

" Oh, you must not make the mistake of calling it a school," said Ethel ; " madam would be shocked at the bare mention of the word. You must know that it is a refined and exclusive home for a few fortunate young ladies. Madam considers it an absolutely safe place for us. I imagine the people around this home think it is a sort of asylum for those who are mentally diseased. They must surely think that we are in some degree dangerous, since we are so carefully guarded."

" It must relieve your friends of a good deal of anxiety," said Gerald, amused at her recital. " Do you have good teachers ? "

" The very best," answered Ethel, " with the exception of the French teacher ; madam is looking for another."

" I know of one. A Parisian, of fine education and elegant manners ; one whom I can heartily recommend," said Major Apthorpe, eagerly. "If you will give me Madam Leonard's address, I will write to her at once, for I am interested in this young man, and would like to get him employment."

"Is he young and handsome?" asked Ethel. Again she noticed the curl of the sensitive lip, as he answered: —

"He is both young and fine-looking."

"Oh, well, that settles the matter," said Ethel, decidedly. "He won't do at all. Madam Leonard had an applicant just before the holidays, and I heard her say to Miss Carpenter, concerning him: 'He had the highest testimonials as to character and ability, but he is too young, a good deal too young, and too good-looking. Young ladies are very impressionable.'"

"Poor young man," said Major Apthorpe, laughing.

"Poor young ladies, you should say," answered Ethel. "We are not allowed to look at a man under sixty, and not even at sixty, if he happens to be a handsome man. But I do wish you would interest yourself in this matter, for I want the girls to have a better

teacher than they have had. But, remember
that you must not only find a man who is
ugly, but he must have commonplace ugliness.
There must be no mystery about him, either.
Nothing picturesque, for there is a wonderful
charm about anything mysterious, and picturesque ugliness has a horrible fascination for
us."

"My friend might arrange a hump, and
limp a little," suggested Gerald.

"But you forget that madam is a woman.
She would be sure to find him out at once,"
said Ethel.

"So women are never deceived?" said he.

"Not when they resolutely set out not to
be," said Ethel. "Sometimes they fail through
carelessness, and sometimes they permit themselves to fall in love, and so are blinded; but
Madam Leonard is constantly on the alert,
and as to her falling in love, why, the idea
is quite too preposterous to think of for a
moment. Her body is fashioned on the
refrigerator plan, in which her heart is laid
away to keep. No, your applicant must be
genuine."

And so they talked, sometimes gravely and sometimes gayly, until Mr. Apthorpe's return, who, hearing them talking so amicably together, said to his sister, in a well-pleased tone of voice : —

"They seem to be getting on. I say, it would n't be a bad plan for Jed to settle down, eh ? "

They saw a good deal of each other during the last week of Ethel's visit. Gerald was beginning to understand her better, and he seemed to seek her society, and she often found herself listening for his step, which she had learned to know. She had not only entirely forgotten to be ungracious, but she was conscious of a spiteful feeling, that was wholly feminine, against Nana Cleveland, who had so entirely misrepresented him, and who, she now felt sure, secretly admired him. She had neglected her father since Major Apthorpe's return, and she promised herself that she would make up for it after she went back to Madam Leonard's. But she really had nothing to write about. She had expressed her admiration of Mr. Apthorpe in the strongest terms, and there was nothing new that she could say. To be sure, she had been to the theatre, and visited some picture-galleries, and had driven about with Mrs. Amesbury and her youngest brother, — that was all ; but she had never kept even the slightest thing from him, and when she had quite made up her mind about Major Apthorpe she would write about him. She had enjoyed her visit extremely, and as the day of her departure drew near, she found herself wish-ing that it might be prolonged. She was to spend the last few days of her vacation with Kitty. Mrs. Amesbury and Mr. Apthorpe expressed real regret at her departure, and a request for a few days at Easter. Major Apthorpe was polite, but she would have been better pleased had he been less light and airy in his farewell.

"I have been thinking the matter over, Miss Townsend," he said, "and find that I cannot comply with your request. It is an impossible one. Fancy," he went on, turning to his brother, "she asks me to find for Madam Leonard an educated, refined Parisian who shall be totally uninteresting. I contend that such a being does not exist. I am very sorry," turning to Ethel. " If there is any other way in which I can serve you," with an exquisite bow, " command me."

She thought, as she drove away : —

"He might as well have said ' Good-by. So glad to have met you. I shall remember you for just about five minutes.'" And she made a firm resolve at that moment to think of nothing but her books and her father on her return to Madam Leonard's.

The days went slowly by. Ethel had enjoyed her visit too much to forget it. The contrast with her present life was too great, but she set herself resolutely at work. She was more studious and more serious than she had ever been before, and Kitty marveled at the change in her. But at last the Easter holidays came, which were of a week's duration only, as Madam Leonard preferred closing the year the first of June. Ethel went home with Kitty as usual, and she spent two days with the Apthorpes. Gerald was away, and did not return until after her departure ; and,

much as she enjoyed Mr. Apthorpe's society,
there seemed to be something wanting. His
brother fumed and scolded because he did
not come back as he had promised, and
Ethel was ashamed to confess, even to herself, how much she missed him. She began
to long for the end of the school year, when
she would go into the country, and forget
everything in the enjoyment of nature.

CHAPTER XIII.

ALLIANCE.

THE social harmony existing in this place was remarkable. As a proof of it here was Fraternity Hall, and there the Amity Club rooms, and a little farther on the church sociable parlors. It boasted three Shakespeare clubs, and book clubs without number. There was sometimes a little disaffection, to be sure, but that is unavoidable among women. For instance, one would-be ruler of society, who had often been heard to declare that she "hated po'try," was offended because she was not chosen president of a Shakespeare club, and withdrew in high dudgeon. This would never do. The Widow Wyse, the unanimously elected president, took it on herself to anoint the creaking wheels of the literary society with the convenient, oleaginous compound she never allowed herself to be without. She insisted upon resigning in favor of the irate lady, which so mollified her that she readily accepted the second place. So peace was restored, and the rightful president more honored than before. It was the fashion to have literary tastes and aspirations, and Alliance would not allow itself to be behind the times. To be sure, the young girls yawned behind their fans at the English literature lectures, and fancied themselves undetected. But now and then a courageous girl would say honestly that she hated the whole thing.

"For goodness' sake!" said one gay young girl to Mrs. Wyse, "is this never to end? I am sure I cannot bear it much longer; I do hope there is no intention of forming a 'Summer School of Philosophy,' but I begin to fear it."

"You poor, little rosebud," answered Mrs. Wyse; "I do pity you, and I shall propose an adjournment until the autumn at our next meeting. I expect a friend from Boston next week—a Miss Cleveland. She is bright and clever, and I am sure you will all like her. You girls must help me entertain her. It is almost time for picnics and excursions. I noticed a new building on the shore of our beautiful little lake. Is it a hall? We might have dancing."

"Oh! yes," answered the young lady. "It is especially for summer picnics, where we may go for shelter. We can dance or do anything else we like."

"How perfectly lovely!" said Mrs. Wyse. "It supplies a long-felt want. Now, do not forget to tell the girls all about it, and we will meet at the clubroom and talk it all over, and plan for the summer; at least, the first part of it. I suppose most of us will be away during July and August."

Miss Cleveland did not reach Alliance until the last week in May, and after her arrival a round of gayeties was begun, which was continued until the last of June, when everything of the kind came to a sudden stop.

Miss Cleveland was enjoying her visit immensely. Mrs. Wyse and her mother spared no pains to be agreeable. The fascinating widow was not surprised to receive an early call from her guest's cousin, Reginald Cleveland, and his friend, August Brenner, the

young German. Indeed, she would have felt
very much disappointed had they not come,
for they had been assigned parts in the pro-
gramme she had arranged. She received the
young men in a flatteringly cordial manner,
and Reginald Cleveland said :—

"I had no idea, Mrs. Wyse, that Alliance
was such a pretty place. We are on our way
North, but we have resolved to stay a day or
two and look it over."

"Oh, that will be charming! but you have
seen nothing of its beauties, which lie in its
surroundings. We shall be more than delighted to point them out to you," said the
fair widow, flashing a smile at Brenner, which
electrified him.

She was dangerously attractive at times, and
she knew well her power over the young German. She had not told her mother the truth
concerning him ; for she knew perfectly well
that there was nothing that could induce him
to leave his native country while she remained
in it. She reasoned that one excuse was as
good as another, until she got ready to explain
everything. She had spoken of him, as she

said, because she wished him to be cordially
received by her mother.

"We must treat our friends to a drive
around our beautiful little miniature lake to-
morrow morning," she said to Nana; "and I
am sure they will be so enchanted that we
shall be able to persuade them to stay until
Friday, for we are to have a picnic in the lovely
grove on Thursday, and they may fish, row,
dance, or do anything else they like; and last,
but not least, there will be several remarkably
pretty girls, whose acquaintance they will
make," looking persuasively at Brenner.

Nana looked up, surprised, for they had
planned to go to an entirely different place
on that day; and Mrs. Wyse, suddenly recol-
lecting it, said:—

"It was a pet plan of my own, and was to
be a surprise for you, my dear; but you see I
had to tell you in order to tempt these young
gentlemen to stay for it."

The truth is, it was an impulsive determi-
nation on Mrs. Wyse's part, formed at the
moment of speaking. Of course, both young
men declared that no such inducement was

necessary. They were only too glad to be
invited to stay. They had started out for a
pleasure trip, and had plenty of time to enjoy
everything as they went along.

They were very enthusiastic in their expressions of admiration of the beauty of the scenery
as they drove around the pond the next morning, which was, indeed, charming. The road
was through lovely woods, through which
glimpses of its shining waters were seen all
the way. In one place the small trees had
been cut down to form a grove, and there had
recently been erected a building, with a small
hall in the second story, and some rooms below
fitted up for the convenience of pleasure
parties.

It was a gay affair that the Widow Wyse
had arranged for the following Thursday. The
young ladies were all charmed by the fair
young German, whose good-nature seemed
inexhaustible. His laugh rang out over the
water, as clear and joyous as a child's. Indeed, he was as unlike the typical German as
one could possibly imagine. He had a smile
and a gay word for all. Only once did his

face become cloudy. He had tried in vain for a *tête-à-tête* with the fair widow, and when he saw her stray off with Colonel Gilroy, a man whom he distrusted the first moment he saw him, he could not bear it, and started off alone in the opposite direction, but not until Mrs. Wyse had, looking back, caught sight of his face. She was not prepared to give him up, and she knew better than to try him too far; so she sauntered on a little way with the gallant colonel, and managed to turn him over to one of the young girls, and strayed back alone, as if by accident, to where young Brenner was sitting apart from, and out of sight of, the others, with a most disconsolate look on his boyish face.

"Ah, you silly boy!" she said, tapping him playfully with her fan. "Do you want everybody to know just how foolish you are?"

"Ah, Julia!" he answered, with tears in his voice, "how cruel you are!"

"No, dear," she answered, caressingly; "but I cannot allow you to make me conspicuous. Come, now, let us go back." And she laid her white hand upon his brow, "to smoothe out the wrinkles," she said.

The ready smiles came back at that warm touch, and he exclaimed, in a transport of joy : —

"Heart's dearest, forgive me ! You are an angel, and I will never doubt you again."

"Never doubt that I am your friend, August," she answered.

"My heart craves something more than friendship," he said, in low, passionate tones, as they started back from whence they came.

"There, now, you are beginning again," she said, laughing. "Do you want to drive me off with that horrid Colonel Gilroy? Do be sensible, and go and talk with that pretty girl in blue. She looks as though she wanted to be amused, and," shaking her finger at him, "don't let me have to speak to you again."

He started off, obediently, making a wry face as he did so.

Mrs. Wyse was indefatigable. She planned entertainments for days ahead, and carried them out successfully. The young men still lingered. Reginald Cleveland, to be sure, urged their departure, but Brenner would not listen. The first of June brought Ethel and

Kitty, to visit Mrs. Onslow, and then Reginald had no desire to go. He fell in love with the dear, absurd little Kitty at once. But it was a hopeless passion, for she was a happy, fun-loving child only. To be sure, she was but six months younger than Ethel, but there were years difference in experience and feeling. Lizzie Highgate, too, came home, to add to the circle; but, contrary to the expectations of the girls, she was amiable and modest, and did not try her peculiar fascinations upon the young men. She did her part in the way of entertaining the strangers in a quiet way, very unlike herself, and Ethel said, wonderingly:—

"There is certainly improvement there. I only hope that it may last."

Lizzie told Mrs. Wyse, who inquired for her brother, that he was going to camp out with Jack Fenton and two or three other college fellows during the summer, and would be at home but a few days during his entire vacation.

The new comers were charmed with August Brenner. Indeed, no one could help being. He had recovered from his momentary feeling of jealousy, and was himself again — bright, happy, joyous. "That horrid Colonel Gilroy" could not disturb him again. He gave him not a moment's thought. It is very true that he heard whispers now and then against the fair Widow Wyse; but they did not trouble him. When she looked at him with those innocent blue eyes he could not think her false. She seemed as guileless as a child. She was good and pure and true. She had told him, not in words, but in a thousand ways, that she loved him, and he would not doubt her.

And Ethel and Kitty went with the tide. Mrs. Onslow said, one morning, as they were starting off on some excursion : —

"I believe you came to visit me, young ladies, but I see you only at breakfast and dinner, after which you are too tired and sleepy to talk."

"It will not last much longer, my dear sister," said Kitty : "Nana Cleveland goes to-morrow. Her cousin goes with her, as escort. He will return immediately, and go directly to the mountains, taking Mr. Brenner with him."

"What a happy disposition your German friend has," said Mrs. Onslow, who had seen him several times during his calls upon her guests, and was very favorably impressed by him.

"Yes," answered Kitty, "he is charming, and I should fall in love with him only it would be useless, as he has eyes for nobody but the Widow Wyse. She says his family worship him."

"It is a pity they are not here to prevent his making a fool of himself," said Mrs. Onslow.

Kitty stared at her sister.

"What is the matter with you, Margaret? I never heard you speak like that before. I could imagine Nana Cleveland making that remark, but not you. You must be ill."

"On the contrary," said Mrs. Onslow, laughing, "I feel particularly well this morning. I do not mean to be uncharitable, but I spoke exactly as I felt."

Nana Cleveland went back to Boston, and from thence to Newport. She asked the Widow Wyse to visit her there; but she had planned to visit Nana in Boston, as it suited her better, so she said : —

"Don't ask me, dear ; it will be such a temptation. I have promised mamma that I will go with her to a quiet place among the mountains, and I make it a point never to disappoint her. But you have made us very happy by your little visit, dear Nana, and if, by any chance, I find myself near your charming 'city by the sea,' I shall certainly look in upon you, if only for an hour." Thus leaving the way open for a change in her plans, if she should so desire.

"My dear Ethel," said Mrs. Onslow, one morning, a few days after this, "you will pardon me, I am sure, for speaking plainly. I do not like your intimacy with Mrs. Wyse. I cannot understand why you should take such an interest in her. I believe her to be unworthy your friendship, and that she is not to be trusted. She uses her friends to further her own ends, and I want to put you on your guard with regard to her. I do not think she would try to injure you, unless you stood in her way ; but she would crush you under her feet if she thought that she could thereby raise herself in any degree."

"Thank you, dear Mrs. Onslow, for speaking," said Ethel; "but do not fear for me. I understand her thoroughly. She cannot hurt me."

"But you told Kitty that you liked her" —

"No, pardon me," interrupted Ethel. "I said that I liked to hear her talk, and I do. She amuses me. I said, also, that I knew just where to find her, and I do. If she says that a thing is so to-day, she will swear, by all the gods, that it *isn't* so to-morrow. I have been making a study of her, and find it remarkably interesting. What a story I might write!"

"Oh, if you are writing a book," said Mrs. Onslow, laughing, "I have nothing more to say. Put her in by all means. Only, as truth is stranger than fiction, your readers would not believe what you could say of her. I hear them say now: 'What an exaggerated character.'"

"If I were writing a book," said Ethel, "I should not dare to put in the half I might."

CHAPTER XIV.

"I should think you would tire of this everlasting round of gayety," said Mrs. Houlton, one morning, as her daughter was preparing to go out. "I do not wish to interfere, but it seems to me that you are wasting a good deal of time upon young Brenner. I cannot divine your motive. You must have one, for you are not in the habit of troubling yourself for the benefit of other people. You certainly do not want to marry him, for he must be younger than you are" —

"Don't trouble yourself about my age, if you please, mamma, or I may retaliate," said the amiable Mrs. Wyse. "I don't mind telling you, however, that it is quite possible that I *may* want to marry him. It depends," she added, mysteriously.

"Oh, Julia!" said her mother. "You cannot be so foolish. He is too young for you, and you know nothing about him. He seems educated and refined, but he is probably an adventurer after your money."

"Ha! ha! ha! I positively cannot help laughing. '*After my money*'! That is very good indeed." Then after a pause, she said : "I do wish, mamma, that you would allow me to manage my affairs in my own way. I did not spend two years abroad for nothing. August Brenner belongs to a family of wealth and eminence, and he is fairly worshiped at home. That ought to satisfy you as far as he is concerned. I married Archibald Wyse to please you. I shall marry a second time to please myself."

"Now, Julia," said her mother, "you are very unkind. I should like to have you tell me what you would have done without Archibald Wyse's money. You certainly would never have seen Germany."

"I was ungenerous," said Mrs. Wyse, seeing that her mamma was really pained. "I 'll take it all back, and forgive you, although I don't think I should be quite as ready to do so if he had not been considerate enough to make me his widow."

"Oh, Julia!" said Mrs. Houlton. "It is dreadful to hear you talk so. Sometimes you positively shock me."

"Poor mamma," said her daughter, mockingly. "You should be willing to let me tell the truth occasionally. And, as I **am** in the mood for it, perhaps a **little more will not** be amiss. You have doubtless **thought me** very penurious many times during the **last** two years. Being the widow of the *rich* Archibald Wyse, I ought surely to have done something for my impecunious mamma."

"I am sure I have never complained," said Mrs. Houlton.

"Very true, mamma," answered her daughter; "but you have thought it, all the same. Now I am going to give you another shock. I told you one of my pretty little fibs concerning the reason of my return home. I should have remained abroad much longer had I been the wealthy widow that you and my friends think me. Archibald Wyse was not the rich man he was represented to be, and it is absolutely necessary for me to replenish my **purse**. I have thought the matter over, and have come to the conclusion that there is no other way to do it than by marriage. If you can suggest any other way, I shall be infinitely obliged to you. But of one thing you may be sure. If I do marry, I shall not allow myself to be again deceived."

This revelation took Mrs. Houlton's breath away. She could not speak.

"Poor mamma," said Mrs. Wyse. "I am really sorry for you, but I am a good deal sorrier for myself. Now I am going to give you a hint as to what I propose to do. I met Mr. Apthorpe in Paris last year, and again in Boston last winter."

"Mr. Richard Apthorpe?" said Mrs. Houlton. "He is very talented, is he not?"

"Yes," answered Mrs. Wyse, "and, what is vastly more to the purpose, he is very wealthy."

"But he is as old as Archibald Wyse," objected Mrs. Houlton.

"It was not Archibald Wyse's age that I objected to as much as his lack of wealth," said the young widow, laughing.

"But is not Mr. Richard Apthorpe pretty high game for you?" said her mother.

"No slang, if you please, mamma," said her daughter. "We must cultivate the graces to the utmost. The only reason that I consented to go to a quiet place with you this summer was to get time to read his books. It will almost kill me, but I shall do it. Thank my lucky stars, I have a tolerable memory. Perhaps they will disclose a weak spot to me. Then my assault will be the easier. I suppose you have been rather tried this summer, but you have behaved beautifully, and you shall not regret it ; I have only a few days more in which to enjoy my flirtations with August Brenner and Colonel Gilroy " —

"You should have nothing whatever to do with Colonel Gilroy, Julia," said Mrs. Houlton. "You know that he is thoroughly unprincipled."

"Never mind, mamma," said Mrs. Wyse ; "as long as he is received into the same society as ourselves it won't do to quarrel with him ; but you need not be troubled ; I couldn't marry him, for he is as poor as a church mouse. I shall not carry it too far. Only just far enough to pique the charming

August. I shall prepare for a vigorous cam-
paign in the autumn. You think I am aiming
too high, but what if I win?"

"Heaven grant that you may!" piously
remarked Mrs. Houlton; "but, on the other
hand, what if you fail?"

"Then," answered the fair Widow Wyse,
"I still have my blue-eyed August."

Poor August! He had entered the door,
which had been left open, the morning being
very warm, and had heard every word of the
last part of the conversation. He would have
scorned to listen, but a remark from the woman
he loved concerning himself compelled him
to pause. He was so completely astonished
that he had not the power to move; as she
ceased speaking, however, he gathered up his
strength and went noiselessly out, hardly
knowing or caring which way he went. He
walked slowly in the direction of the beautiful
pond, upon whose bosom he had spent so
many happy hours. Soon he quickened his
pace, and, with feverish eagerness, hurried on,
looking neither to the right nor to the left.

Mrs. Wyse, glancing out of the window, saw

him leave the house, and, catching a glimpse of his face, in which despair was plainly written, turned to her mother, and said, excitedly : —

"Oh, mamma! it was August. He must have heard. What shall I do? Don't speak," putting her hand to her head. "Let me think." Then, after a pause, she started up, saying, "Ring for Ninette. There is no time to lose."

"Ninette, my hat and wrap; and tell Thomas to bring around the carriage at once."

"But, my love," said the elder widow, alarmed, "think what you are doing. Where are you going?"

"Don't be silly, mamma," answered her daughter; "I am not going to drown myself." (Was it intuition that made her say that?) "I am simply going to call upon Miss Townsend; and I want you to remember that poor August was very fond of her, and that, whatever happens, I am not to blame."

Mrs. Houlton noticed that she spoke of the young German in the past tense.

"It is an omen!" she exclaimed. "Something dreadful is going to happen. I never saw Julia so excited."

"You little dear!" exclaimed Mrs. Wyse, enthusiastically, as Ethel came down to greet her visitor. "What a charming color you have!"

Then, turning to Kitty, she went on, archly : —

"If our blue-eyed German could only see her now he would be more distracted than ever."

"Why do you say that, Mrs. Wyse," said Ethel, "when you know perfectly well that it is you he admires ?"

"And you know perfectly well that it is you he admires," mimicked Mrs. Wyse. "It is only poor me who hears his secrets. Ah, you little coquette! you will make him do something desperate yet. He has been perfectly wild ever since you came."

Then she added, more seriously : —

"Don't play with him, dear, for he is a nice fellow, and I am very fond of him. I knew him in Germany, you know."

"What nonsense you are talking !" began

poor Ethel; but Mrs. Wyse interrupted her by
saying : —

"Now tell me all about your visit with
whom Nana Cleveland calls 'that delightful
old roaring lion,' you fortunate girl. I have
not had time to ask you before."

"She has well named him, Mrs. Wyse,"
said Ethel, coldly; "for he is the king of men,
as the lion is the king of beasts."

"And his brother, too, is very charming, is
he not?"

This was too much. Ethel had striven to
be polite since her visitor's first absurd hints
with regard to August Brenner; but now she
was ice itself, as she answered : —

"Everybody was very kind to me at Mr.
Apthorpe's; but I saw so little of his brother
that I cannot satisfy your curiosity with regard
to him."

The Widow Wyse saw that Ethel was in no
mood to be trifled with, so she began to talk
to Kitty. She soon took her leave, however,
saying, —

"I see you are dressed for a drive, so I will
not detain you."

From Mrs. Onslow's Mrs. Wyse drove directly to see her dear friend, Lizzie Highgate; and, during their long, confidential chat, she assured her feminine admirer that it was her solemn belief that Ethel Townsend was amusing herself with poor August Brenner, who was desperately in love with her.

"Nonsense!" said Lizzie; "he has eyes only for you. Ethel Townsend is undoubtedly pretty, but she lacks your agreeable manners; and August Brenner is a young man of discernment."

"That shows what a perfect little goose you are, Lizzie," said the agreeable Mrs. Wyse. "He knows that I am his friend. I have told him so many times, and he naturally confides in me; but it is only as a friend, and so you may inform anybody who speaks of this matter. You ought to know me better than to suppose, for an instant, that I would encourage him in any such foolishness were he inclined to show it, which, I assure you, he is not. Please to understand, Lizzie, once for all, that there is not a particle of truth in your surmise. I have been annoyed by hearing the same thing from Ethel

Townsend herself; but I understand it perfectly, coming from her, and so I have just
told her. It is simply a blind. But from you
it is different."

"I am very sorry," said poor Lizzie. "I did
not understand it; and I shall take pains to
correct the general impression wherever I go."

This was exactly what the Widow Wyse
expected and desired; and she started for
home, satisfied with her morning's work.

"I believe that my head aches too badly to
drive this morning," said Kitty, as Mrs. Wyse
left the house.

"Then I will not go," said Ethel; "but,
instead, will bathe your head and try to cure it.
I am a good deal of a doctor."

"Oh, no!" said Kitty. "Gertie will be disappointed if you do not go. I shall lie down
for a little while, and if I can get a half-hour's
sleep, my head will be all right."

So they started off.

"Where shall we go, dear?" asked Ethel of
the little girl.

"Wound the pond," answered she.

"'Wound the pond' it shall be," as she
gave the order to the coachman.

When they reached the woods he was told to drive more slowly, that they might enjoy the cool shade. Ethel descended from the carriage many times to gather ferns and wild flowers, which grew in abundance everywhere, for her young friend. Gertrude was a bright, merry, little thing, and was very fond of Ethel, who thoroughly enjoyed her small companion's artless talk. She was a revelation to her. Being wholly unaccustomed to children she was amazed to find her so clever of speech.

"Now you must tell me which you think is the prettiest view, and I will tell you which I think is the prettiest," said Gertrude as they drove along.

"Very well," said Ethel, amused and looking eagerly about. Soon they came to an opening in the woods, through which were lovely glimpses of the water.

"Stop a moment, James," she said. "I think it would be hard to find a finer view than this."

"It is very pretty," said the child, "but I think there is a prettier one."

"Drive along then," said Ethel, "and we will find it." They soon began an ascent.

"Now, when we get to the top of this hill," said the child, confidently, "you will see it."

"You are right," said Ethel, as they reached the place, "for we can not only see the water, but the fields and mountain beyond."

"Yes," said Gertrude, "I knew you would say so. I like that mountain. I 'should like to be way up on the top of it. I could touch those white clouds and I could see all over the world, could n't I ? "

"Not quite so far as that, dear," answered Ethel, " but I am sure you could see a great distance. The view from the top must be grand. But we must not linger here, or we shall not be back in season for luncheon, and my little girl must be hungry ; besides, these pretty flowers are beginning to droop."

As they reached the bend in the road nearest the pond, Ethel noticed two men leaning over the prostrate form of another. She stopped the carriage, fearing that something was wrong and that assistance might be needed. She descended from the carriage and walked quickly toward the spot. One of the men, seeing her, raised his hand warningly, but it was too late.

She gave a low cry of horror as she recognized in the white, upturned face the features of August Brenner. She staggered as though about to fall as the man caught her and led her back to the carriage just as two men drove up.

"There is the doctor, miss," said the man. "We have done all we could for him, but I am afraid it's of no use."

"Oh, can't you do something, Doctor?" said Ethel, appealing to him in agonized tones. "You *must* do something for him!"

"Yes, yes, child, I'll do all that mortal can," said he, recognizing her as Mrs. Onslow's guest. Then to the coachman: "Take her home at once," and hurried to the drowned man.

How Ethel got home she did not know. She saw nothing but August Brenner's white face and fixed, staring eyes.

Mrs. Onslow found her, a few minutes after her return, leaning against a marble statue, herself almost as white as her support. Her clenched hands and wild, frightened eyes alarmed her hostess. She put her arms tenderly around her, saying, —

"Ethel, dear, what is it? Can't you tell me?"

Ethel made an effort to speak, but she could not, and for the first time in her life she fainted, losing consciousness entirely.

The news spread like wildfire. Ninette, who was out with her pets, heard of it before Mrs. Wyse's return, and she met her mistress, who seemed greatly excited, with red, swollen eyes. He had been kind to her, and she had had little enough of real kindness in her life, heaven knows! She poured forth a volume of mingled French and English, and much to Mrs. Wyse's discomfort ended by calling that lady a murderess.

Mrs. Wyse's voice was very unsteady, as she said : —

"I don't know what you mean, Ninette, but you have been impertinent before, and I have overlooked it, but I shall bear it no longer. Go to your room at once and prepare to leave me!"

"Vary well, madame. I s'all find some ozer place. Adieu, madame," and with a mocking courtesy she left the room.

Mrs. Wyse turned to her mother and said, passionately :—

"To think of Ninette's proving ungrateful, after all I have done for her ; but I have borne too much from her, and I shall be glad to get rid of her."

"But, my dear," said her more politic mother, "are you wise in sending her off like this? It seems to me that it is a poor time to do it. There are plenty of ladies who will be glad of her services. She will have no difficulty in finding another place, and she knows it very well; and you can imagine what she will say of you. You know best, of course, what you want to do. I only offer the suggestion."

"You are right," said her daughter, wearily. "If I could only send her back to Paris; but she will not go, and she will make me all the trouble she can. There was never anybody as hardly used as I have been."

And she burst into a passion of tears.

To tell the truth, the events of the last few hours had so worn upon her nerves that she could not control herself, and she fell upon the sofa in violent hysterics.

Mrs. Houlton ran this way and that for restoratives. She was very much frightened, and rang sharply for Ninette; but no Ninette appeared. She rang again and again to no purpose, and she was forced to go for her. She found her in her room, putting various things into her boxes.

"Why do you not come when I ring for you?" demanded Mrs. Houlton, indignantly.

"I am no longer in madame's service," said Ninette, proudly.

"How can you be so unfeeling when she has done so much for you?" said Mrs. Houlton, half crying. "She is ill,—dying, perhaps,—and I don't know what to do for her."

On hearing this, Ninette softened and ran quickly down to her mistress. They loosened her clothing, and rubbed her cold hands, giving her cordials as soon as she was able to swallow.

Mrs Wyse did not often indulge in this particular kind of weakness, and Ninette was frightened also. After she had fallen into an uneasy slumber, Mrs. Houlton improved the opportunity to say:—

"You were very cruel to say what you did, Ninette. You see," she went on, confidentially, "that, being an old friend, this young man's death will be very hard for her to bear. And to think of your accusing her of being the cause of it! It is not true, and I cannot think why you should have imagined it."

"Oh, I am vary sorry!" said the tender-hearted Ninette. "It was vary wicked. I will beg madame's pardon."

"No," said Mrs. Houlton; "it will be better to say nothing about it. She was so excited at the time that she probably will not remember it, and I am sure it would make her worse to bring it all back again. Do not speak of it, even, and, above all things, Ninette," said the wily woman, "promise me to say nothing to anybody else of your foolish suspicions. It would injure her a good deal if you did."

"Nevare, nevare!" said Ninette, solemnly.

Mrs. Houlton sent the maid out of the room to fetch something, when she saw signs of her daughter's awakening, and whispered to her, hurriedly:—

"Say nothing to Ninette. Treat her as usual."

And when that repentant person came back and asked, tenderly, "How does madame find herself?" Mrs. Wyse answered : —

"Better, thank you. You are a good girl, Ninette, and I shall not forget it. You need not stay now. You must be tired. Mamma says that you have done everything for me. You had better go out and take the air; it will do you good."

"Madame is vary kind," said Ninette, withdrawing.

And so peace was made; and a few days after, Ninette might have been seen standing before her little mirror, admiring herself, as well as some pretty articles of jewelry which her mistress had just given her.

Ethel was prostrated by a low, nervous fever, the result of the shock she received on that fatal day.

"What a dreadful woman!" she exclaimed, in speaking of the sad event for the first time. "Poor August! he was innocent as heaven, and she as false as hell."

"Don't think about it, dear," said Mrs. Onslow, soothingly.

But she could not help it. His love was so pathetic, and his death so tragic.

"I thought I knew her," she said; "but I did not. I could not conceive of a woman so false, so base."

She had overheard enough of their conversation to understand perfectly his feelings toward her, and she felt sure that her cruel deception was the cause of his death.

Hearing Mr. Onslow say to his wife, "Mr. Reginald Cleveland will take charge of the body," she said, with quivering lips:—

"How strange, how horrible, to speak of one so lately full of life and joyousness, as 'the body'!"

"It is dreadful, Margaret!" said poor Kitty, tearfully, when she found her sister alone. "Do you suppose she did really care for him? I heard her moaning and sobbing in her sleep, last night. She will die if she goes on so."

"I do not quite understand it, dear," answered her sister. "I hope she will be better when she gets away from this place. The doctor said this morning that she must go as soon as she is able to travel. You must take her home, and let her have rest and quiet."

"Kitty, dear," said Ethel, a few days later, "what was said in the papers of this dreadful — accident?"

"Oh! there were long notices of it," answered Kitty, "and a good many surmises; but it seemed to be the general opinion that he slipped from the rocks near where they found him."

"Please send the papers to papa. I cannot write about it, and I should like him to know," said Ethel. After which the subject was dropped, and not mentioned again.

Mrs. Wyse called before Ethel went away. She was paler than usual, and seemed quite subdued.

"How is the poor child?" she asked of Mrs. Onslow. "I am so sorry for her. It is dreadful for us all, but particularly so for her. May I see her?"

"I do not think that she will feel equal to seeing you this morning; but I will let her know that you are here," said Mrs. Onslow, leaving the room.

"Ethel, dear," she said, on reaching the chamber, "Mrs. Wyse is below, and wishes to see you. What shall I say to her?"

"Oh, I cannot see her!" said poor Ethel, "and you must tell her so. Her name, even, causes a feeling of suffocation here," putting her hand on her heart.

It was a sad ending to her otherwise pleasant visit; and as she said good-by to Mrs. Onslow, she felt that she should never again see her in her lovely country home.

Ethel and Kitty spent two months of perfect rest and quiet. Mrs. Brewster felt that they had had excitement enough for the summer, and she gave up all thought of entertainments for them. Ethel slowly recovered her strength, and as that came back, her spirits in a measure returned, though she felt that she should never be quite so light-hearted as she had been. She had learned a lesson which she would never forget. She had long talks with Mrs. Brewster, who endeavored to bring her out of the morbid state into which she had fallen.

"Of what are you thinking, my dear?" asked Mrs. Brewster one morning, seeing a far-off look in her eyes. "It isn't good for a young lady to think too much."

"It would be better for some of us, if we

thought more than we do," answered Ethel.
" I was thinking, as you spoke, how strange it
was that the world should applaud what I
believe it should wholly condemn. Am I uncharitable? I believe some of my friends
think me so, but if I am, I must have had
wrong teaching all my life. I wish I did not
begin to analyze people as soon as I meet
them, but I cannot help it. I have been taught
to hate any thing low or base or false, and if
I detect a false note in the music of a person's
conversation, it shocks my moral nerves. A
lie is no less a lie because it has a fanciful
dress of words. I was taught that a lie is an
intention to deceive, and that a person may
tell a falsehood without uttering a syllable.
An example comes to my mind now. One
day last summer Mrs. Wyse gave Lizzie
Highgate to understand by her manner that
a certain story was true, when she knew perfectly well that it was not. I remonstrated
with her, and she answered, laughing at her
own shrewdness: 'I am not responsible for
what Lizzie Highgate thinks. I did not say a
word.' Now, I contend that she was respon-

sible. That, by her manner, she deliberately deceived Lizzie. She did not want her to know the truth."

"Well, my dear," answered Mrs. Brewster. "We must take the world as we find it, and not quarrel too much with poor, weak, human nature. Mrs. Wyse is a woman of the world, and she has a certain pleasing manner which makes her popular. It is not necessary to be literally and painfully truthful, at all times. We must be as charitable as possible."

"If I must say that a black lie is the white truth in order to be thought charitable," said Ethel, vehemently, "I would rather be thought otherwise. God gave me clear, perceptive faculties, good eyesight, and acute hearing. Does He wish me, think you, to go through the world with my eyes half closed, with cotton in my ears, and my mind clouded with fancies? It is quite true, as you say, that Mrs. Wyse is a woman of the world, and that the world admires her and thinks her clever. Heaven preserve me from ever becoming a woman of the world!"

"My dear child," said Mrs. Brewster,

laughing, "you should go into the lecture
field. You would be invaluable to the cause
of universal suffrage, should you undertake to
advocate it."

"That is just what I was going to speak
about," said Ethel, eagerly: "why do not these
earnest women, with clear heads and strong
minds, take up this matter, and try to raise
their frail sisters to the dignity of true woman-
hood? They labor and strive and agonize in
their endeavor to gain the right to vote.
What would the ballot be in the hands of
such a woman as the Widow Wyse?"

"What you say is quite reasonable," said
Mrs. Brewster, "but are you ready to begin
to revolutionize the world of women?"

"Yes," answered Ethel, laughing. "I have
already begun, and I believe I have made one
convert."

"Nevertheless," said Mrs. Brewster, "you
must allow me to say that I fear that you are
a little too sweeping in your denunciations.
To borrow your own words, 'A lie is an
intention to deceive.' We cannot always
understand motives."

"It would be impossible to put one's self quite in another's place," said Ethel, thoughtfully. "Do you mean that I should say, always, 'That would be a lie if I said it, but from her standpoint it may be the truth'? Is that what you call being charitable?"

"You are incorrigible, my dear," said Mrs. Brewster, laughing.

"At least I am in earnest," said Ethel. "But, dear Mrs. Brewster, I cannot see the justice of exaggerating the good I see, and of covering with the mantle of charity the evil. If I am impartial on the one hand, why should I not be on the other? I don't mean that evil should be sought for, by any means, but how can I help seeing what is so plainly on the surface? It is not jealousy, I am sure, which prompts me to speak so. I seem to feel differently from most girls I meet. I have always associated with older people than myself, and I am not used to petty dealings. Possibly they seem worse to me on that account. Mrs. Wyse said to me last June: 'What a popular girl you might be if you chose,' and I answered: 'Possibly, if I would allow myself to be all things to all people.'"

"'Oh, no!'" she said. "'If you would only allow people to love you.' Now, I am perfectly willing to be loved," she went on, laughing, "but I must be loved for what I am. I will not seem to be what I am not. To quote the Widow Wyse again in this connection. She says that she 'would rather have the goodwill of a dog than the illwill of one,' while I feel prompted to say, 'I would rather that a dog, even, should feel that he must offer me clean paws to shake.' I have been trying to reason this out lately, but I have hardly come to a satisfactory conclusion concerning it."

"Don't try any more now, dear," said Mrs. Brewster, seeing that she looked pale and tired, "but go out for a drive. It will do you good. The carriage is at the door and Kitty is just coming down."

CHAPTER XV.

In September Ethel went to Newport to visit the Apthorpes. What a change from the quiet of the country. In the picturesqueness of its scenery, its attractive exclusiveness, its deliciously green lawns, its wealth of flowers and vines, the bewildering brilliancy of the scenes along the fashionable drive, to say nothing of the architectural beauty of its buildings, this charming "city by the sea" stands unrivaled. How many times Ethel exclaimed during her too brief stay, "It is the loveliest place in the world!"

She was necessarily quiet, for she had not fully recovered her strength. Her friends were very careful of her, but she took long, delightful drives, and it was like a glimpse of paradise to sit on the broad piazza and listen with a strange, intense delight to the music of the voice which sang in her heart and brain long after its owner had left her alone.

"You have been ill," he would say, "and you must let me amuse you. I have nothing else to do." His voice took a tenderer tone when addressing her. Was it only because she had been ill, or did he really care?

Ah, Gerald Apthorpe, take care! Do you know that you are playing upon heartstrings? Touch that sweetly-tuned instrument softly. Those are not cold wires you are sweeping your hand across, but quivering nerves that are sensitive only to your touch. Lightly, my dear fellow, lest you shatter that delicate organ, and stain your white hand with the life-blood that runs only for you!

This every-day association was very dangerous to Ethel's peace of mind. The time flew by on swift wings. She had been too happy. The last day had come.

"Well," said Gerald, cheerfully, "this is your last day. I hope you are feeling quite strong and well again." How her heart sank. What a delusive dream it had all been.

The Widow Wyse made a hasty trip to Newport. She said to her mother before she set out: —

"Ethel Townsend dislikes me, and I am afraid of her. She is too good for this wicked world. It is a pity that her wings should not grow a little faster. I am sure that I, for one, could spare her without a sigh. She has too much influence altogether with the Apthorpes to suit my purposes. I must try to weaken it."

"But how can you do that?" asked Mrs. Houlton. "Do be careful, Julia; remember"—

"Let bygones be bygones, if you please, mamma," said her daughter. "I acknowledge myself human. I sometimes make mistakes, but I know what I am doing now."

She arrived at the Ocean House at night, and the next day she took a carriage at the fashionable hour for driving in order to reconnoitre, taking care to be veiled so as not to be recognized. She peered eagerly into every carriage she passed, and soon sank back as if wishing to be unnoticed as Mr. Apthorpe's black horses dashed by. The carriage contained Major Apthorpe, his sister, and Ethel. Mrs. Wyse gave an order to her coachman, who drove rapidly to Mr. Apthorpe's house. Fortune favored her. He was at home.

"I came, Mr. Apthorpe," she said, in a low, sympathetic voice, "to see poor, little Ethel, or, at least, to hear from her. How is she?"

"Much better," he answered. "She has nearly recovered. She has been quite ill."

"Oh, yes!" she said. "I know all about that unfortunate affair. It was a dreadful shock to her. It was hard for all of us, but particularly so for her. I don't think she cared for him, but he was terribly in earnest, and she liked him so much that he was deceived, and when he found" —

"What on earth are you talking about, Mrs. Wyse?" interrupted Mr. Apthorpe. "I don't understand, in the least, what you mean. Who was this young man, and what had he to do with Ethel?"

"Oh, don't you know?" said Mrs. Wyse with well-assumed surprise. "I thought you knew. Of course I ought not to speak if she has kept it from you. She would not like it. She used to be very fond of me, but since this dreadful event" —

"I must insist upon your explaining, Mrs. Wyse," said Mr. Apthorpe, losing patience.

"It was poor August Brenner, who was drowned. Oh, I don't know how to tell you!" and Mrs. Wyse put her handkerchief to her eyes.

"Do you mean young Cleveland's German friend?" asked Mr. Apthorpe. "I read about it at the time. Do you mean to tell me that the young man drowned himself — committed suicide, on Ethel's account?" he asked, with cruel distinctness.

"Oh, don't put it in that way!" she protested. "It is too dreadful. He slipped in perhaps — but Ethel is so tender-hearted. I am sure she did not intend any harm, but I suppose she thought that she might have unconsciously encouraged him."

"If you mean to tell me that Ethel Townsend encouraged, and then deliberately jilted, any young man, all I can say is I don't believe it!" he answered, with warmth.

"Oh, Mr. Apthorpe!" she said, appealingly, "I am sure I did not say that. I did not mean it; I love Ethel, and would do anything in my power to make her happy," and her blue eyes filled with tears.

"Well, well!" said Mr. Apthorpe, softening, "perhaps you did not. I love Ethel, too, and what you said excited me. I beg your pardon."

"My dear Mr. Apthorpe," said the fair widow, "I am so sorry for this. I feel very much to blame, but how could I know? Pray, do not tell Ethel that I have spoken about the matter. I naturally thought you would know about the cause of her illness, and with the best of motives came to inquire about her. Do not tell her that I have been here, even. It might do harm. Promise me that you will not, Mr. Apthorpe, or I shall be very unhappy."

"No, I will not," he answered, and she left him a little in doubt as to whether she had done her cause any good. She had to leave it, she profanely said, "In the hands of Providence."

Mr. Apthorpe said nothing to Ethel, but he told his sister what Mrs. Wyse had told him, but he expressed doubts as to its truthfulness, although it was very evident that his informant believed it he said, and he ended by saying, decidedly : —

"Of course you will say nothing to Ethel about it, and, above all things, say nothing to Jed. It might influence him."

And Gerald Apthorpe moved gently away from the door he was about to enter, saying to himself, —

"So that is their pet plan. That Dick, of all men, should turn matchmaker. How I should like to laugh at him. Poor little Ethel! I wonder if it is true."

CHAPTER XVI.

THERE was a dull, heavy pain in Ethel's heart as she left her kind friends for Madam Leonard's. She had now no doubt as to the extent of her folly, for every heartbeat said " Gerald, Gerald, Gerald." She had been cast out of paradise. Everything seemed wanting.

" Why could I not have heeded the warning that was given me? " she said. Yet she did not blame him. She did not believe that he was the coldly selfish being that he had been represented. She simply felt that he could not care for her. She cared for nothing, not even her father. She might have been cast upon a desert island for all the sympathy she had for those around her. She longed to hide herself from everybody, and she had almost resolved to write and beg her father to come and take her away, when something occurred to make her forget herself and her troubles for the time being. What it was the reader will

learn in the following letter, addressed to her
father : —

"My Dear Papa, — Something dreadful has
happened.   The house is shaken to its very
centre. Madam Leonard is ill, and has taken
her bed.   Miss Carpenter goes about the house
like a madwoman, and Miss Eliza looks white
and   horror-stricken.   Everybody   seems   to
have lost her wits, and my own hand trembles,
as you can see.   I hear you ask, 'What is it
all about?'   You would never guess, so I must
tell you, but prepare to be shocked.   Lizzie
Highgate eloped from the house last night with
Jack Fenton. Our Jack! Only think of it!
And the sly girl pretended that she did not
know him.   Her roommate found a note in
one of her books, addressed to Madam Leonard this morning, which said that before she
should receive it they would be married and far
away.   Everything had been planned with the
greatest care.   Her trunks had been packed and
left so that they might be sent, without trouble,
to her home.   She deceived her roommate by
saying that her mamma was ill, and that she

was going to put a few things into her trunk
fearing that she might be sent for in haste.
She had put in everything she had, excepting
the few things she took with her. She must
have thrown her hat, wrap, and satchel out of
the window, for the servants say that she did
not have them with her when she passed
through the kitchen and out of the back door.
They supposed that she returned to the house
by another way. Poor Jack! How could he
be so foolish? He will never be able to respect
himself, or her. It was his third year in college, and he might have graduated with honor.
Why could he not have waited and married in
a respectable kind of way. I do not believe
that her family would have tried to prevent it,
for Jack is not a young man to be easily
refused. But I understand the matter perfectly.
It was wholly Lizzie's affair. She could not
afford to wait. She was too much afraid of
being found out. She cannot control her
temper, and she is very well aware of it. I am
too much disgusted just now to pity Jack as
much as he deserves, but poor, dear, refined Mrs.
Fenton. It will be a terrible blow to her, for

she idolizes Jack.　I know she will try to love his wife, but how can she?　If she were more teachable I am sure so much gentleness and refinement would have a softening effect upon her, but I am very much afraid that Lizzie's vulgar ideas of money, her tawdriness and slatternly ways, will be a sore trial to her mother-in-law.　I understand now those mysterious visits to the country during vacations.　I shall write again soon.　Dear papa, how I wish I were with you.

"Your loving

" TEDDY."

Ethel, as I have said, forgot herself in the general excitement.　And it really was a benefit to her.　After a few days the girls settled down to their books.　Madam Leonard appeared once more among them, and feeling that some reference must be made to Lizzie's flight, said : —

"Young ladies, you all know of the disgrace that Miss Highgate has brought upon herself and upon this house, and I only speak of it to ask you not to discuss it among yourselves, but to forget it as soon as possible. She is not worthy of your thoughts."

Ethel applied herself more closely to her studies than ever, and the time went slowly by until another Thanksgiving day arrived. It was just a year since her first visit to Boston. How much had happened since then! How old she felt. She went home with Kitty, and divided the time between the Brewsters and the Apthorpes. She soon learned that the Widow Wyse was in Boston.

Her mother had said before she left her : " I am afraid you are going to be disappointed, Julia. You know that Boston does not open its arms to strangers readily, and you have few acquaintances there."

" You forget, my dear mamma, that instead of stopping at a hotel, as I have generally done, I am to visit Nana Cleveland. You don't half know your daughter. Sometimes she sees years ahead. Do you remember calling me foolishly impulsive because I interested myself in a poor lecturer a few years ago? Do you know why I did it? No? Well, I will tell you. As I was coming home from Madam

Leonard's, one vacation, I overheard Professor
Scamore, a man of letters, and a severe critic,
say (he was sitting in front of me with another
gentleman) that Mr. Follansbee was sure to
make his mark, and that, within a short
time, men of culture would be proud to
acknowledge him as a friend. Chance threw
him in my way. You know what I did. It
was very little. I simply talked him up.
Wrote, asking him to give a course of lectures.
The girls sold the tickets and he had a fine
audience. I bought a ticket and went to one
of the lectures, during which you had to
pinch me to keep me awake, if you remember,
and I was ill or out of town during the others;
but he was very grateful to me, all the same.
I have a letter upstairs, in which he pours
forth volumes of gratitude, and says that, if he
can ever serve me in any way, he shall be
glad and proud to do it. He was poor and
dependent then : now he has influence among
people whom I wish to know, and I purpose to
let him serve me."

"Julia," said Mrs. Houlton, admiringly, "I
will never attempt to give you advice again.

You are thoroughly capable of taking care of yourself."

Attentions were showered **upon** her through the influence of Nana Cleveland and Mr. Follansbee, and Mrs. Houlton took infinite pains to inform the social world of Alliance that dear Julia was "quite the rage in Boston."

"You as are changeable as a chameleon, Mrs Wyse," said Mr. Apthorpe, one evening, as they met at an art reception, and **the** fair widow was fluttering from one to another.

"Oh, Mr. Apthorpe, don't say **that**," she answered. "I am as steadfast **as** the sun. The fact is," she went on, with pretty hesitancy, and a flash of **her** white teeth, "I am dreadfully afraid of you, and don't **do** myself justice. I have been intensely interested in your writings, but I find **such** soarings into the clouds, such divings into the very depths, that I get lost in trying to follow you. Still, knowing a little, I find myself desiring to know more, and to understand better, **and I** come to you with 'Explain, explain!' upon my lips. 'Come down to my poor comprehension,' but, before I can gain courage **to speak, you** — **you**" —

"Oh, I growl, I suppose," he said, laughing.

"Yes, yes!" she answered, eagerly. "You *do* growl *at me*, only I never should have dared to say so."

And Ethel, looking on from a distance, said bitterly to herself:—

"Is it possible that this man of learning, wit, talents, everything that goes to make up what the world acknowledges a superior in all respects, should take pleasure in listening to that shallow woman's flattery. It cannot be!"

Kitty was intensely amused.

"Do you know," she said, approaching Ethel, "that the Widow Wyse is making eyes at your Mr. Apthorpe?"

"I know that she is trying to make a good impression upon him, and I am afraid she has succeeded," said Ethel.

"If she should succeed in capturing him, a pretty life he would lead her after he found her out," said Kitty, laughing.

"You don't say that you think she wants to marry him," said Ethel, aghast. "How perfectly absurd."

"Absurd or not," answered Kitty, "it is precisely what she is aiming at. I don't know where your eyes have been that you have not seen what is plain to everybody."

Ethel's face was a study. This was what she had never dreamed of.

"She shall not deceive him!" she said fiercely to herself. "I will speak first. It will be my duty to expose her."

Then a flush of shame swept over her, at the thought of speaking against anybody, even the Widow Wyse. What right had she to prejudice anybody against her? Mr. Apthorpe could surely look out for himself. She made up her mind to wait, and if she found that what Kitty had said was really true, and that he was blind to her defects — why, then! he should have a hint, if no more.

"Her soul is not large enough to appreciate him," she thought, indignantly. "An eminent writer says: 'The meanest nature can comprehend the evil in which it shares, but it requires, to judge a lofty one, to be on a level with it. Only Alp can talk to Alp.' How can that poor little molehill talk to this grand, mighty Alp?"

She was lost in thought when Mr. Apthorpe, making his way to where she stood, silent and alone, said to her, in a low tone : —

"That's right, dear. When you have that look, I know just what you are doing. I am sure that that is not a look of admiration you are casting upon the Widow Wyse. You are dissecting her at this moment, taking her to pieces, unjointing her members, taking out her heart " —

"Oh, no!" interrupted Ethel at this point, "I was only trying to find if she has one. I am inclined to think that she has, and that it is in a petrified condition, so I have to work carefully, so as not to spoil my fine instruments."

Mr. Apthorpe laughed; then he said, more seriously : —

"Beware of her, my dear; she seems amiable, but she has a well-filled quiver at her back. Her arrows are pretty things to look at, daintily covered and ornamented, but they are pointed with steel and dipped in the poisonous saliva which moistens her tongue."

"Oh! I am so glad you can read her," said

Ethel. "I did n't want to speak, but I felt that I must."

" I am very sorry you should think me dull," he answered, dryly. The absurdity of which remark made Ethel laugh again.

" Ethel, dear," said Mrs. Wyse, fluttering up to her at this moment, " I have been looking for you everywhere, to tell you that Nana is to have a reading at her house to-morrow afternoon at four. There are to be only a few people, and each one is to recite something from his or her favorite poet."

She saw refusal in Ethel's face, and she went on, persuasively : —

" You must come, dear, for we cannot get along without you. I am sure it will be pleasant, as it is to be like those we had last summer in Alliance, which we enjoyed so much."

" How can she refer, in the remotest degree, to the events of the summer?" thought Ethel, who changed her mind suddenly, and answered : —

" Thank you, I shall be very happy."

" You dear girl," said Mrs. Wyse, effusively,

"and you will be prepared to recite something, I am sure; and Mr. Apthorpe, too, if he will honor us so much," she said, beaming upon him. "I am sure you will be amply repaid by listening to Ethel's exquisite voice."

"Yes," answered Ethel, quickly, giving him a meaning look. "I should like to have Mr. Apthorpe there. He has never heard me read, even."

"What assurance," thought Mrs. Wyse. However, she was thankful for his ready acceptance, and said : —

"How perfectly charming to have you both. I am sure that Nana will be as much delighted as I am."

A celebrated elocutionist first recited a gem from Longfellow, and sat down amid great applause. Then, as if for contrast, Ethel thought, the Widow Wyse, who was the moving spirit of the affair, called upon Miss Townsend. She looked unusually pale, and the widow said to herself : —

"She is nervous; she will break down, and serve her right, too. It will teach her to be less confident."

But there was no sign of tremor in Ethel's voice as she rose and said : —

"I will recite 'The Well's Secret,' by John Boyle O'Reilly."

She began, and in a light, joyous manner recited the first two verses : —

> "'I knew it all my boyhood; in a lonesome valley meadow,
>   Like a dryad's mirror hidden by the wood's dim arches near:
> Its eye flashed back the sunshine, and grew dark and sad with shadow,
>   And I loved its truthful depths, where every pebble lay so clear.

> "'I scooped my hand and drank it, and watched the sensate quiver
>   Of the rippling rings of silver, as the drops of crystal fell;
> I pressed the richer grasses from its little trickling river,
>   Till at last I knew, as friends know, every secret of the well.'"

Then her tone and look changed to surprise, which deepened, and finally turned to horror, as she finished the next two verses, with her eyes fixed upon the Widow Wyse : —

"'But one day I stood beside it, on a sudden, unexpected,
When the sun had crossed the valley, and a shadow hid
the place:
And I looked in the dark waters, saw my pallid cheek
reflected,
And beside it, looking upward, met an evil, reptile
face:

"'Looking upward, furtive, startled at the silent, swift
intrusion:
Then it darted toward the grasses, and I saw not where
it fled;
But I knew its eyes were on me, and the oldtime sweet
illusion
Of the pure and perfect symbol I had cherished there
was dead.'"

Mrs. Wyse shuddered, and seemed to shrink
within herself as Ethel went on, with clasped
hands and a tone and look of inexpressible
sadness:—

"'Oh! the pain to know the perjury of seeming truth
that blesses!
My soul was seared like sin to see the falsehood of the
place
And the innocence that mocked me; while in dim, unseen
recesses,
There were lurking fouler secrets than the furtive,
reptile face.

"'And since then—ah! why the burden? When the
    joyous faces greet me,
With eyes of limpid innocence, and words devoid of
    art,
I cannot trust their seeming, but must ask what eyes
    would meet me
Could I look in sudden silence at the secrets of the
    heart?'"

There was no **applause.** Everybody was
hushed to silence. After a moment Mrs.
Wyse said, with a little, uneasy laugh:—

"That was almost too realistic, Miss Townsend. You looked as though **you** saw the
serpent."

"I did," said Ethel, turning her dark eyes
once more upon **the** Widow Wyse; "and I
saw, too, the **soul it had** lured to destruction."

There was a painful silence, and all felt
relieved when Nana came to Mrs. Wyse's
rescue with a lighter selection. But the fair
widow was beginning to feel that she was
playing a losing game. She knew that Ethel
Townsend thoroughly understood her; but she
had hoped for silence on her part. Her re-
sources were infinite. **She was, to** all appear-

ances, an enthusiastic, impulsive creature, with the kindest possible heart; but her schemes were deeply laid, and often successfully carried out. She would tell a deliberate falsehood with such a charmingly innocent air that no one who was a stranger to her could doubt its complete truthfulness.

CHAPTER XVII.

FAREWELL TO MADAM LEONARD'S.

AFTER her return to Madam Leonard's, Ethel dragged on a few weeks, and then, in sheer desperation, wrote to her father, begging him to come to her.

"I cannot stay here any longer, dear papa," she said; "I feel so miserably ill and unhappy. You must come and take me away."

"Poor little Teddy!" he said, compassionately; "I had no idea that she was especially fond of Jack. Foolish fellow! he deserves his fate, however bad it may be."

He telegraphed for a passage home, and traveled day and night to reach the port in season for it; but before he embarked he cabled a dispatch to his daughter, that she might not be in doubt as to his response to her appeal.

He had a quick passage, and hurried at once to Madam Leonard's. He was troubled to find Ethel looking so pale and thin; and after making his arrangements to take her away, he left for Mobile, taking Dido and the solemn Dumps back to their Southern home. His business there was hastily dispatched, and he came back to his daughter, who would have started at once for New York could she have had her own way; but she did not propose it, for she could give no satisfactory reason for not calling upon the friends who had been so kind to her.

"I met my old friend, Dick Apthorpe, in Boston, my dear," said her father, "and promised to spend the night with him. We will go directly there; and some time during the day we will pay a visit to your kind friends, the Brewsters. I feel very grateful to them, and hope some time to be able to make some return. I only wish that your friend Kitty might accompany us now."

But Ethel did not echo the wish. She only wanted to be alone with her father, and away from all her old friends. It was necessary for her to forget. She did not dare to think of her visit to the Apthorpes, for she felt that it would be utterly impossible to say good-by to Gerald without betraying herself.

It was hard to say good-by to Kitty, who was almost inconsolable.

"Why did you come if you must go away so soon?" said the weeping girl. And Ethel said to herself:—

"Alas! why did I?"

Happily for her, Major Apthorpe was away. On learning this, Ethel tried to throw off her depression, and she succeeded in a degree. It was hard parting from Mr. Apthorpe. She had wound herself so completely around his heart that he felt that she belonged to him.

"Hang it, Ned," he said, dashing the tears from his eyes, "I am as fond of Ethel as you are. Why must you take her away? I could almost wish I had never seen her."

He was as savage as a bear for the next few days.

When Major Apthorpe returned and learned of Ethel's departure, he experienced a feeling of disappointment, an odd sense of loss that he could hardly understand.

"I thought she was to stay with Madam Leonard through the year. What is the cause of her sudden departure?" he asked his sister. "I am sorry to have missed seeing her."

"It was a great surprise to us," answered Mrs. Amesbury. "Her father came home unexpectedly, and finding her far from well, decided to take her abroad at once. Dick is greatly disappointed. His rheumatism is worse than ever."

Gerald smiled. This convenient rheumatism often occasioned a smile between the sister and younger brother. Gerald found his brother in one of his "moods," and accosted him with :

"Well, old fellow, how are you? Eleanor says that you have a touch of rheumatism. Can I do anything for you?"

"Thank you, for nothing," growled Mr. Apthorpe. "I should like to know how the devil you always manage to be away when I want you most? I particularly wanted you to meet Dr. Townsend. You said you would be home last week."

"Oh, come, now," answered Gerald good-naturedly, "don't bite my head off. How was I to know that you wanted me? I'll go and bring them back by force if you say so."

Mr. Apthorpe smiled, a little grimly, it is true, but he could not long withstand his favorite brother's sunny nature and they were soon discussing matters of interest to them both, when suddenly Richard Apthorpe turned to his brother and said, abruptly : —

"Well, Jed, what do you think of Ethel Townsend?"

"Everything that is pleasant," he answered. "I told Eleanor just now that I could not remember meeting a more charming young lady."

"I don't think you can," said the elder brother, with unnecessary vehemence, "and what is more I don't think you ever will."

"Poor girl," said Gerald softly. "I hope she may be able to forget, in time, her grief, or remorse, whichever it may be."

"What do you mean?" asked his brother, sharply. "What absurd story have you heard?"

"I heard," said Gerald, smiling a little sadly, "what you said to Eleanor on the subject, at Newport."

"I do not believe the story," said Mr. Apthorpe, earnestly, "and you should not. I believe it was made out of whole cloth by that infernal mischief-maker, the Widow Wyse."

"Do you know the cause of her illness?" queried Gerald, pointedly.

"How should I know?" burst forth his brother. "Good heavens! You seem to think — you and the Widow Wyse — that a young girl can't be ill without being able to trace back the cause to some silly love affair."

"At all events," answered Gerald, "she does not care for me, so, my dear brother, put that idea out of your mind, and we will say no more about it."

He had a little time at his disposal, and, strange to say, he did not know what to do with it. It was strange how he missed Ethel. She fairly haunted him. If she had been at Madam Leonard's, he probably would not have thought of her. He strayed down town and into a picture-gallery. There was a fine portrait of a young girl, by a celebrated artist, before him, and he fell to criticizing it and comparing it with Ethel, and his verdict was very much in the latter's favor. He remembered the exact curve of the golden-brown eyelash. The exact tint of the soft flush of the fair, young cheek. The exact shape of the graceful,

willowy form. Yet he was not in love with
her. He took pains to assure himself of this
fact. Oh, no! He admired her, it is true,
and he wished there were more like her. The
world would be better, brighter, fairer — that
was all.

CHAPTER XVIII.

DOCTOR TOWNSEND took Ethel directly to Nice, where he determined to stay until she was stronger, when they would travel about, in the hope of taking up her mind and restoring her spirits.

"Don't ask me any questions, papa," she had said to him. "I shall tell you all about it some time, but not now." And he had respected her wish. She grew happier and more like herself as the weeks went by. Her father was so tender and so devoted to her that she felt that, since other love was denied her, he should have all that she could give him. He was the best guide that she could have had. In the first place, he knew perfectly his daughter's tastes. Then he was thoroughly familiar with the places they visited, and he had delightful and influential friends everywhere. Ethel knew that she ought to be happy, but she felt that fate had been strangely cruel to her in throwing her into the society of the only man who had the power to spoil her life. They went to Paris, intending to spend some weeks, but on the second day her father came in hurriedly, and told her that she **must** prepare to leave for Ecouen that afternoon.

Ethel demurred, and was disposed to **ask** questions, but her father silenced her by saying that there was a young American artist with whom he had business, staying there, and it was absolutely necessary for them to go. He was so unlike himself that her curiosity was greatly excited. He did not want her to leave the house, but she said : —

"I must, papa. You know that I have made an engagement with some of your friends to drive this morning. You desired me to go, and I cannot well excuse myself now."

He let her go reluctantly, and looked at her curiously when she came back. She saw that he did not wish to be questioned, so she was silent, but she wondered greatly what whim had seized him. He was uneasy until they started, when he seemed **like** himself again,

but Ethel noticed that he talked rather more
rapidly than usual, as if he still feared questions. He entertained her with anecdotes
and stories all the way. Her mind was so
taken up with his unusual manner that she
forgot everything else, but the next morning
she recalled the pleasant drive of the day
before, and she said, suddenly : —

"Papa, whom do you suppose I met during
my drive, yesterday? You would never be
able to guess, so I will tell you. It was our
runaways, Jack Fenton and his wife. I was
glad to notice that they looked a little shame-
faced as they recognized me. How queerly you
look at me, papa. Do tell me what it is; I
never knew you to act so strangely before."

"Oh, it is nothing," he answered, with an
uneasy laugh. "I knew they were in Paris,
but I thought you would not care to meet
them, so I " —

"So you did not say anything about it,"
finished Ethel. "Well, I think you might
have told me. I don't object to meeting them
at all. Why should I? Of course I dis-
approved of their running off in that indecent

manner, and I did n't like Lizzie, but I could n't cut such old friends as the Fentons. Why, Jack has always seemed like a brother to me. You would not want me to refuse to notice them, would you ? "

" No ; oh, no ! " he answered ; " but I thought " —

" Thought what, papa ? Do tell me what you thought ! "

" Why," said poor Dr. Townsend, " I thought that you were fond of Jack" —

" And so I am," said Ethel. " I have just told you so."

" But I thought you cared so much that this marriage " —

" You thought I was in love with poor old Jack ! " said Ethel, understanding for the first time the cause of her father's uneasiness. " And so you hurried me off to this little place for fear I should meet him. Oh, you foolish papa ! that is really too good ! " and she went off into peals of laughter which did his heart good to hear. He had not heard her laugh since she left her Southern home for Madam Leonard's.

"I did n't think you could tell such an awful fib. Where is your artist with whom you have business?" she asked.

"It was no fib at all, my dear. I saw him this morning, but the business was more important to him than to me, as he wanted me to let him have some money;" and they were very merry the rest of the day.

"To tell the truth, papa, I was very much disappointed in Jack. I wanted him for Kitty; it would have been such a suitable match in every way. Ah!" she went on, with a sigh, "I shall never try my hand at matchmaking again." Then, after a pause, she said, mischievously: "So you are called 'the handsome American,' in Dresden?"

"Who has been talking nonsense to you, my dear?" answered Dr. Townsend.

"The Widow Wyse," replied Ethel. "Why have you not spoken of her? I want to know how she struck you."

"She did n't strike me," said her father, laughing.

"Oh! but she tried to, I am sure of it," said Ethel. "You are actually blushing. Come, now, confess that she tried to fascinate you, and that I have had a narrow escape from a step-mother."

"How absurd!" answered her father. "Why should a pretty young woman try to fascinate an old fellow like me?"

"I shall not allow you to call my papa names," said Ethel, with mock severity. "What will you say when I tell you that this 'pretty young woman' tried all her arts upon your dear friend in Boston last winter?"

"What! not Dick Apthorpe? You can't mean him, surely!" said her father, laughing heartily at the idea. "A pretty life he would lead her after he found her out!"

Ethel clapped her hands.

"That is precisely what Kitty said," she answered. "I never dreamed of such a thing until she suggested it; then it was plain enough — especially after Nana Cleveland told me that she suspected that Julia Wyse was not as wealthy as she was reputed to be, and that she was obliged, much against her will, to economize."

"So your friend is mercenary?" said Dr. Townsend.

"Call her a chance acquaintance, if you please," answered Ethel. "My friends are dear to me."

Dr. Townsend was puzzled. He had been so sure that it was Jack's marriage which had troubled Ethel that he had thought of nothing else. What could it be? At last a thought came to him which, he believed, explained the whole matter. It must have been the young German who was drowned. Ethel had written of his pleasing qualities, and had sent papers giving an account of his death; but she had not spoken of the tragic event in her letters, or made any reference to him since they had been together. That was unnatural: everything was clear to him now. Poor child! Well, he must try and make her forget. After all, a dead sorrow was better than a living one. He was glad to know that it was not Jack.

CHAPTER XIX.

THE winter was wearing away. Gerald Apthorpe was busier than ever. He was up early and retired late; and this sort of life began to tell upon him. His sister remonstrated.

"You are burning your candle at both ends," she said. "It is not like you to do that. What is the matter with you? You are growing reckless. I think a change would do you good."

He turned her off with a laugh; but he knew that what she said was true. He grew nervous and irritable, and was as unlike the Gerald of old as it was possible to conceive. Finally he resolved to go abroad again. His friends did not oppose it: in fact, they urged him to go. After he had made up his mind, he was feverishly anxious to be off.

"If you should run across the Townsends," said his brother, "you have my leave to bring them back, as you suggested."

"It is not likely that I shall," answered Gerald. "I have no idea in what part of the world they may be."

"I had a letter from Ned last week which told me that they would be in Paris next month," said Mr. Apthorpe, eagerly.

"Ah," said his brother, carelessly, as he went out; "I will look them up, perhaps."

"'Perhaps'! you insensible piece of flesh and blood," snarled Mr. Apthorpe, as the door closed upon him. "'*Perhaps*'!"

But Major Apthorpe was not so indifferent after reaching Paris. He hastened to their hotel, only to find that they had just left for Ecouen. He lost no time in setting out for that place, and found, to his chagrin, that they had returned to Paris. He said to himself: "What a fool I am! I am even worse than Dick." But he made up his mind, nevertheless, that he would find them, if he had to follow them all over Europe. He went back to Paris, and on reaching the hotel again, learned that they had gone out.

"At all events," he said to himself, "they are here;" and for want of anything else, he went to the Louvre, and, strolling around, he came upon a familiar figure standing before the picture of "Cupid and Psyche," by Girard. It was Ethel, and she was lost to everything but the contemplation of that first kiss of love. He came softly and stood beside her until the consciousness of a familiar presence aroused her, and she turned expecting to see her father. She uttered but one word, "Gerald," but the tone was so full of love, the face was so full of happiness, that he could not mistake it. His heart gave a joyful bound.

"Ethel, dear," he said, in the low, caressing tones she knew so well, "bless you for that name and that tone. Ah, you cannot take it back," as she drew her hands away blushing. "Love cannot be deceived. I shall always be 'Gerald' to you now." And he cabled this message to his brother: —

"I shall bring them back as I promised."

CHAPTER XX.

FOILED.

If Gerald Apthorpe had grown nervous and irritable, Nana Cleveland had grown still more so. She was positively snappish. It is strange how long a woman will hope against hope, in matters of the heart, grasping at the least straw floating past her. She knew that Major Apthorpe was utterly indifferent to her, and yet she could not banish him from her thoughts. She was impatient for the departure of her visitor, who had already made an unconscionably long visit, but she could hardly tell her to go, although she felt that her indebtedness had long since been canceled. The Widow Wyse seemed in no hurry to go home. She bore the shafts of Nana's ready wit with smiling composure, or with innocently inquiring eyes. But she could not deceive that young lady. Nana was far too clear-sighted for that, and she was annoyed by her guest's behavior. She had done her best for the friend who had so pleasantly entertained her in the summer, but she felt that Mrs. Wyse was not the success in Boston society that she promised to be on her first introduction to it. Indeed, it seemed to be quite the fashion to smile whenever her name was mentioned. The widow herself was conscious that she was not getting on, and that had made her reckless. Her mysterious visits to nobody-seemed-to-know-where were exasperating to Nana, who was frankness itself.

Mrs. Wyse had many stormy scenes with herself in the privacy of her own chamber, where she laid plans only to reject them. She had met Mr. Apthorpe "accidentally," she had told Nana, several times, but she had made no advances in his good graces, and, driven desperate by her non-success, which she believed to be due to what Ethel Townsend had been pleased to say against her, she resolved upon a bold stroke, which was to again "beard the lion in his den." In other words, to pay him a visit and try and explain Ethel's dislike in a way which would be creditable to herself. She was a good actress, and she felt that she must succeed. She *would* succeed. Accordingly, choosing the morning on which she knew Mrs. Amesbury would be engaged in mission-work, she dressed herself carefully, and came downstairs, saying sweetly to Nana : —

" I should ask you to go with me, dear, but I have a little tiresome business to do, and it would bore you." Then, with moistened eyes, she impulsively seized Nana's hand, saying, "This has been such a charming, charming visit, dear Nana, I have stayed longer than I ought." She hurried away, while Miss Cleveland said to herself : —

"Thank goodness, you think of leaving at last! but, my lady, I propose to know where you are going this morning. It is nasty business ; but I feel justified in doing it." And hastily donning hat and wrap, she followed her.

The widow's heart beat fast as she rang Mr. Apthorpe's doorbell. It was an audacious movement, and she could not foresee the result. Mr. Apthorpe came smilingly toward her. He had just received his brother's dispatch, and was in high good-humor. Mrs. Wyse was flattered. She was herself again.

She looked up timidly, then dropped her eyes quickly, and something like a blush overspread her features as she gently pressed the hand he offered her.

"Oh, Mr. Apthorpe!" she began, in a hesitating way, ''I am leaving Boston"—here her voice faltered perceptibly — "and — and — I could n't go without seeing you again. I hoped you would call — but"—

"Well, well! sit down, madam, sit down. What can I do for you?" he said, in a bluff voice, which was hardly encouraging. He was saying to himself, "What the devil brings Becky Sharp here this morning?"

"Are you angry with me, dear Mr. Apthorpe? I know I ought not to have come; but I have enjoyed your society so much — and — and — oh, Mr. Apthorpe! I *could n't* go away without saying good-by," and here she put her handkerchief to her eyes; but, feeling that he was growing impatient, she uncovered them and went on. "I want to explain something to you before I go. I feel that I have been misrepresented. Ethel Townsend used to be very fond of me; but since last summer

—I was not to blame, indeed I was not; and it was so — cruel — to — misrepresent me to *you*. If it had been anybody else I should not care; but I do want you to understand me."

"Zounds, madam! do you take me for a fool?" he burst forth, angry that she should speak thus of Ethel. "I do understand you perfectly. I have understood you for a long time, and — hang it! I shall say something I ought not say to a woman if this goes on." And he strode out of the room with something on his lips that sounded very much like a d—n.

The Widow Wyse looked ten years older when she returned to her friend's house than she did when she set out from it. Nana met her, with a pale face and set lips.

"I think, Nana," she said, wearily, "that I must go home to-morrow."

"You have come to a wise resolve," said Nana, in clear, cutting tones. "When my guest so far forgets herself as to make her efforts to capture a rich husband so evident that it becomes the subject for club gossip, it is time for her visit to end. You have evidently been refused this morning."

"You have been playing the spy!" said Mrs. Wyse, roused to sudden anger.

"I saw you enter Mr. Apthorpe's door, if that is what you mean," answered Nana, coolly. "And as *I* have business, also, to-day, it is doubtful if I am able to see you again. I will send Wilson to assist you in your preparations for leaving. Allow me to wish you a very good-day, and better success another time." And sweeping her a mocking courtesy, Nana left the room.

And the Widow Wyse went back to her precious mamma.